T0272893

The Gates
of Morning

The Gates of Morning

Henry De Vere Stacpoole

MINT EDITIONS

The Gates of Morning was first published in 1925.

This edition published by Mint Editions 2021.

ISBN 9781513283807 | E-ISBN 9781513288826

Published by Mint Editions®

MINT
EDITIONS

minteditionbooks.com

Publishing Director: Jennifer Newens
Design & Production: Rachel Lopez Metzger
Project Manager: Micaela Clark
Typesetting: Westchester Publishing Services

The Gates of Morning

Henry De Vere Stacpoole

The Gates of Morning was first published in 1925.

This edition published by Mint Editions 2021.

ISBN 9781513283807 | E-ISBN 9781513288826

Published by Mint Editions®

MINT
EDITIONS

minteditionbooks.com

Publishing Director: Jennifer Newens
Design & Production: Rachel Lopez Metzger
Project Manager: Micaela Clark
Typesetting: Westchester Publishing Services

Contents

BOOK I

I

The Canoe Builder

Dick standing on a ledge of coral cast his eyes to the South.

Behind him the breakers of the outer sea thundered and the spindrift scattered on the wind; before him stretched an ocean calm as a lake, infinite, blue, and flown about by the fishing gulls—the lagoon of Karolin.

Clipped by its forty-mile ring of coral this great pond was a sea in itself, a sea of storm in heavy winds, a lake of azure, in light airs—and it was his—he who had landed here only yesterday.

Women, children, youths, all the tribe to be seen busy along the beach in the blazing sun, fishing with nets, playing their games or working on the paraka patches, all were his people. His were the canoes drawn up on the sand and his the empty houses where the war canoes had once rested on their rollers.

Then as he cast his eyes from the lagoon to the canoe houses his brow contracted, and, turning his back to the lagoon he stood facing the breakers on the outer beach and the northern sea. Away there, beyond the sea line, invisible, lay Palm Tree, an island beautiful as a dream, yet swarming with devils.

Little Tari the son of Le Taioi the net maker, sitting on the coral close by, looked up at him. Tari knew little of life, but he knew that all the men of Karolin swept away by war had left the women and the boys and the children like himself defenceless and without a man or leader.

Then, yesterday, from the northern sea in a strange boat and with Katafa, the girl who had been blown to sea years ago when out fishing, this strange new figure had come, sent by the gods, so the women said, to be their chief and ruler.

The child knew nothing of whom the gods might be nor did he care, alone now with this wonderful new person, and out of earshot of his mother, he put the question direct with all the simplicity of childhood.

"Taori," said little Tari, "who are you?" (*é kamina tai*)

Could Dick have answered, would the child have understood the strange words of the strange story Dick might have told him? "Tari, I come of people beyond the world you know. My name is Dick Lestrange, and when I was smaller than you, Tari, I was left alone with an old sailor man on that island you call Marua (Palm Tree), which lies beyond sight fifty miles to the north. There we lived and there I grew to be a boy and Kearney, that was his name, taught me to fish and spear fish, and he made for me things to play with, little ships unlike the canoes of the islands. And then, Tari, one day long ago came Katafa, the girl who was blown away from here in a storm. She lived with us till Kearney died and then we two were alone. She taught me her language, which is the language of Karolin. She named me Taori; we loved one another and might have lived forever at Marua had not a great ship come there filled with bad men, men from the eastern islands of Melanesia. They came to cut the trees. Then they rose and killed the white men with them and burned the ship and in our boat we escaped from them, taking with us everything we loved, even the little ships, and steering for Karolin, we came, led by the lagoon light in the sky."

But he could not tell Tari this, or at least all of it, for the very name of Dick had passed from his memory, that and the language he had spoken as a child; Kearney, the sailor who had brought him up, was all but forgotten, all but lost sight of in the luminous haze that was his past.

The past, for men long shipwrecked and alone, becomes blurred and fogged, for Dick it began only with the coming of Katafa to Marua, behind and beyond that all was forgotten as though consumed in the great blaze of tropic light that bathed the island and the sea, the storms that swept the coconut groves, the mists of the rainy seasons. Kearney would have been quite forgotten but for the little ships he had made as playthings for the boy—who was now a man.

He looked down at the questioning child. "I am Taori, Tari tatu, why do you ask?"

"I do not know," said the child. "I ask as I breathe but no big folk—madyana—will ever answer the questions of Tari—Ai, the fish!" His facile mind had already dropped the subject, attracted by the cries of some children, hauling in a net, and he rose and trotted away.

Dick turned his gaze again to the north. The question of the child had stirred his mind and he saw again the schooner that had put in to Palm Tree only to be burned by the Melanesian hands, he saw again Katafa and himself as they made their escape in the old dinghy that Kearney had taught him to handle as a boy. He saw their landing on this beach, yesterday, and the women and children swarming round him, he the man whom they considered sent by the gods to be their chief and leader.

Then as he gazed towards the north the memory of the men from whom he had escaped with the girl stained the beauty of sea and sky.

There was no immediate fear of the men who had taken possession of Palm Tree; the men of Palm Tree had no canoes, but they would build canoes—surely they would build canoes, and as surely they would see the far mirror blaze of Karolin lagoon in the sky, just as he had seen it, and they would come. It might be a very long time yet, but they would come.

Dick was an all but blook, a kanaka, a savage, and yet the white man was there. He could think forward, he could think round a subject and he could imagine.

That was why he had sent a canoe that morning across to the southern beach to fetch Aioma, Palia and Tafata, three old men, too old for war, but expert canoe-builders, that was why when gazing at the tribe in full congregation, his eyes had brightened to the fact that nearly a hundred of the youths were ripening to war age, but under all, lighting and animating his mind, raising daring to eagle heights, lay his passion for Katafa, his other self more dear to him than self, threatened, ever so vaguely, yet still threatened.

War canoes! Did he intend fighting any invaders in the lagoon or as they drew towards shore, or did he vaguely intend to be the attacker, destroying the danger at its source before it could develop? Who knows?

A HAND FELL UPON HIS shoulder and turning, he found himself face to face with Katafa, a lock of her dark hair escaped from the thread of elastic vine that bound it, blew right back on the breeze like an eagle's feather, and her eyes, luminous and dark instead of meeting his, were fixed towards the point where he had been gazing—the due-north sea line.

"Look!" said Katafa.

At big intervals and in certain conditions of weather Palm Tree, though far behind the sea line, became visible from Karolin through mirage. Last evening they had seen it and now again it was beginning to live, to bloom, to come to life, a mysterious stain low down in the southern sky, a dull spot in the sea dazzle, that deepened by degrees and hardened till as if sketched in by some unseen painter, the island showed beautiful as a dream, diaphanous, yet vivid.

With her hand upon his shoulder they stood without speaking, their minds untutored, knowing nothing of mirage, their eyes fixed on the place from which they had escaped and which was rising now so strangely beyond the far sea line as if to gaze at them.

They saw again the horde of savages on the beach, figures monstrous as the forms in a nightmare, they felt again the wind that filled the sail as the dinghy raced for safety and the open sea, and again they heard the yells of the Melanesians mad with rum stolen from the schooner they had brought in, and which they had burnt. And there, there before them lay the scene of the Tragedy, that lovely picture which showed nothing of the demons that still inhabited it.

Then as Dick gazed on this loveliness, which was yet a threat and a warning, his nostrils expanded and his eyes grew dark with hate. They had threatened him—that was nothing, they had threatened Katafa, that was everything—and they still threatened her.

Some day they would come. The vision of Palm Tree seemed to repeat what instinct told him. They would build canoes and seeing the lagoon mirror-light in the sky, they would come. They had no women, those men, and here were women, and instinct half whispered to him that just as he had been drawn to Katafa, so would these men be drawn to the women of Karolin. They would scan the horizon in search of some island whose tribe might be raided of its women and seeing the lagoon light they would come.

Ah, if he had known, danger lay not only to the north, but wherever greed or desire or hatred might roam on that azure sea, not only amongst savages, but the wolves of civilization.

To Dick there was no world beyond the world of water that ringed the two islands; no Europe, no America, no history but the history of his short life as the life of Katafa, and yet even in that life, short as it was, he had learned to dread men and he had envisaged the foundation of all history—man's instinct for war, rapine and destruction.

Then gradually the vision of Palm Tree began to fade and pass, suddenly it vanished like a light blown out and as they turned from the sea to the lagoon, Katafa pointed across the lagoon water to a canoe approaching from the southern beach.

It was the canoe Dick has sent for the canoe builders and, leaving the coral, they came down to the white sand of the inner beach to meet it.

II

THE REVOLT OF THE OLD MEN

Two women were in it, and as they drove it ashore beaching it with the outrigger a-tilt, Dick, followed by Katafa, approached, and resting his hand on the mast stays attached to the outrigger gratings, he turned to the women, who, springing out, stood, paddles in hand, looking from him to Katafa.

"And the builders?" asked he, "where are they?"

The shorter woman clucked her tongue and turned her face away towards the lagoon, the taller one looked Dick straight in the face.

"They will not come," said she. "They say Uta Matu alone was their king and he is dead, also they say they are too old. 'A mataya ayana'—they are feeble and near past the fishing, even in the quiet water."

The shorter woman choked as if over a laugh, then she turned straight to Dick.

"They will not come, Taori, all else is talk."

She was right. The express order had gone to them to cross over and they refused; they would not acknowledge the newcomer as their chief, all else was talk.

Several villagers, seeing the canoe beaching, had run up and were listening, more were coming along. Already the subject was under whispered discussion amongst the group by the canoe, whilst Dick, his foot resting on the slightly tilted outrigger, stood, his eyes fixed on the sennit binding of the outrigger pole as if studying it profoundly.

The blaze of anger that had come into his eyes on hearing the news had passed; anger had given place to thought.

This was no ordinary business. Dick had never heard the word "revolt," nor the word "authority," but he could think quite well without them. The only men who could direct the building of the big war canoes refused to work, and from the tone and looks of the women who brought the message, he saw quite clearly that if something were not done to bring the canoe-builders to heel, his power to make the natives do things would be gone.

Dick never wasted much time in thought. He turned from the canoe, raced up to the house where the little ships were carefully stored and came racing back with a fish spear.

Then, calling to the women, he helped to run the canoe out, sprang on board and helped to raise the mat sail to the wind coming in from the break.

"I will soon return," he cried to Katafa, his voice borne across the sparkling water on a slant of the wind; then the women crouched down to ballast the canoe, and with the steering paddle in his hand he steered.

The canoe that had brought Katafa drifting to Palm Tree years ago had been the first South Sea island craft that the boy had seen. The fascination of it had remained with him. This canoe was bigger, broader of beam and the long skate-shaped piece of wood that formed the outrigger was connected with it not by outrigger poles but by a bridge.

Dick, as he steered, took in every little detail, the rattans of the grating, the way the mast stays were fixed to the grating and how the mast itself was stepped, the outrigger and the curve of its ends, the mat sail and the way it was fastened to the yard.

Though he had never steered a canoe before, the sea-craft inborn in him carried him through, and the women crouching and watching and noting every detail saw nothing indicative of indecision.

Now there are two ways in which one may upset a canoe of this sort by bad handling, one is to let the outrigger leave the water and tilt too high in the air, the other is to let the outrigger dip too deep in the water.

Dick seemed to know, and as they crossed the big lift of sea coming in with the flood from the break, he avoided both dangers.

The beach where the remnants of the southern tribe lived, was exactly opposite to the beach of the northern tribe, and as both beaches were close to the break in the reef, the distance from one to the other was little over a mile. Then as they drew close, Dick could see more distinctly the few remaining huts under the shelter of a grove of Jack-fruit trees; beyond the Jack-fruit stood pandanus palms bending lagoonward, and three tall coconut palms sharp against the white up-flaring horizon.

As the canoe beached, Dick saw the rebels. They were seated on the sand close to the most easterly of the huts, seated in the shadow of the Jack-fruit leaves; three old men seated, two with their knees up and one tailor fashion, whilst close to them by the edge of a little pool lay a girl.

As Dick drew near followed by the taller of the boat women, the girl, who had been gazing into the waters of the pool, looked up.

She was Le Moan, granddaughter of Le Juan, the witch woman of Karolin now dead and gone to meet judgment for the destruction she had caused. Le Moan was only fourteen. She had heard of the coming of the new ruler to Karolin and of his bringing with him Katafa, the girl long thought to be dead. She had heard the order given to her grandfather Aioma that morning to come at once to the northern beach as the new chief required canoes to be built, and she had heard the old man's refusal. Le Moan had wondered what this new chief might be like. The monstrous great figure of Uta Matu, last king of Karolin, had come up in memory at the word "chief," and now, as the canoe was hauled up and the women cried out "He comes," she saw Dick.

Dick with the sun on his face and on his red-gold hair, Dick naked and honey-coloured, lithe as a panther and straight as a stabbing spear. Dick with his eyes fixed on the three old men of Karolin who had turned their heads to gaze on Dick.

Le Moan drew in her breath, then she seemed to cease breathing as the vision approached, passed her without a word and stood facing Aioma, the eldest and the greatest of the canoe-builders.

Le Moan was only fourteen, yet she was tall almost as Katafa, she was not a true Polynesian; though her mother had been a native of Karolin, her father, a sailor from a Spanish ship destroyed years ago by Uta Matu, had given the girl European characteristics so strong that she stood apart from the other islanders as a pine might stand amongst palm trees.

She was beautiful, with a dark beauty just beginning to unfold from the bud and she was strange as the sea depths themselves. Sometimes seated alone beneath the towering Jack-fruits her head would poise as though she were listening, as though some voice were calling through the sound of the surf on the reef, some voice whose words she could not quite catch; and sometimes she would sit above the reef pools gazing deep down into the water, the crystal water where coralline growths bloomed and fish swam, but where she seemed to see more things than fish.

The sharp mixture of two utterly alien races sometimes produces strange results—it was almost at times as if Le Moan were confused by voices or visions from lands of ancestry worlds apart.

She would go with Aioma fishing, and with her on board, Aioma never dreaded losing sight of land, for Le Moan was a pathfinder.

Blindfold her on the coral and she would yet find her way on foot, take her beyond the sea-line and she would return like a homing pigeon. Like the pigeon she had the compass in her brain.

This was the only gift she had received from her mother, La Jennabon, who had received it from seafaring ancestors of the remote past.

Crouching by the well she saw now Dick standing before Aioma and she heard his voice.

"You are Aioma?" said Dick, who had singled the chief of the three out by instinct.

The three old men rose to their feet. The sight of the newcomer helped, but it was the singling out of Aioma with such success by one who had never seen him that produced the effect. Surely here was a chief.

"I am Aioma," replied the other. "What want you with me?"

"That which the woman had already told you," replied Dick, who hated waste of words or repeating himself.

"They told me of the new chief who had come to the northern beach—*e uma kaio tau,* and of how he had ordered canoes to be built," said Aioma, "and I said, 'I am too old, and Uta is dead, and I know no chief but Uta; also in the last war on that Island in the north all the men of Karolin fell and they have never returned, they nor their canoes.' So what is the use of building more canoes when there are no men to fill them?"

"The men are growing," said Dick.

"Ay, they are growing," grumbled Aioma, "but it will be many moons before they are ready to take the paddle and the spear—and even so, where is the enemy? The sea is clear."

"Aioma," said Dick, "I have come from there," pointing to the north; "the sea is not clear."

"You have come from Marua (Palm Tree)?"

"I have come from Marua, where one day Katafa came, drifted from here in her canoe; there we lived till a little while ago when men landed, killing and breaking and burning—burning even the big canoe they had come in. Then Katafa and I set sail for Karolin, for Karolin called me to rule her people."

"And the men who landed to kill and burn?" asked Aioma.

"They are still on Marua; they have no canoes but they will build them, and surely they will come."

Neither of Aioma's companions said a word whilst Aioma stood looking at the ground as if consulting it, then his eyes rose to Dick's face. Age and war had made Aioma wise, he knew men and he knew Truth when he saw her.

"I will do your bidding, Taori," said he quite simply, then he turned to the others, spoke some words to them, giving directions what to do till his return, and led the way to the canoe.

Le Moan, still crouching by the well, said nothing. Her eyes were fixed on Dick, this creature so new, so different from anyone she had ever seen. Perhaps the race spirit was telling her that here was a being of her father's race miraculously come to Karolin, perhaps she was held simply by the grace and youth of the newcomer—who knows?

Dick, as he turned, noticed her fully for the first time and as their eyes met, he paused, held by her gaze and the strangeness of her appearance, so different from that of the other natives. For a moment his mind seemed trapped, then as his eyes fell he passed on and taking the steering paddle pushed off, the wind from the reef-break filling the sail of the canoe.

Le Moan, rising and shading her eyes, stood watching as the sail grew less across the sparkling water, watching as the canoe rose and fell on the swell setting in from the break, watching as it reached the far white line of the northern beach where Katafa was waiting for the return of her lover.

III

The Little Ships

The primitive canoe of the Pacific is a dugout—the trunk of a tree hollowed and shaped into the form of a boat, so narrow in proportion to its length as to be absolutely unstable but for the outrigger.

The outrigger, a long skate-shaped piece of wood fixed to port—always to port—by poles on a central bridge, is an apology to the sea for want of beam, and the sea accepts it—on conditions. But for the outrigger, no canoe of any size would dare the sea, but for it the islands would have been sealed as between themselves, war made impossible, and the drift of people between island and island and between island and continent.

Far away in the remote past some man once stood, the father of this daring invention; little dreaming of the vast consequences of the work to which he had put his hand.

Dick at the steering paddle saw a figure on the northern beach as they drew near. It was Katafa, waiting for him, the wind blowing her girdle of dracæna leaves and her hand sheltering her eyes against the sun. Standing just as Le Moan was standing on the southern beach sheltering her eyes and watching the canoe that carried the first man who had ever made her turn her head.

Some children were playing near Katafa and a fishing canoe was putting out near by, but he saw only Katafa.

"Katafa," said Aioma, who was crouched by the after outrigger pole. "It is she sure enough, and they said she was dead and that her ghost had returned bringing you with her, Taori, but the dead do not return. Katafa, she was the girl under the taboo of Taminan, the girl no man or woman might touch, and then one day she went fishing beyond the reef and a storm took her and she was drowned, so they said."

"She was not drowned," replied Dick. "The wind blew her to Marua where I was—I and another whose face I have near forgotten, Kearney, he was called, and he made canoes but not like these, then one day he went among the trees and did not return. Then the god Nan came to the island and after him the men of Karolin who fought together so that all were killed, and then came the bad men as I have told you and would have killed us but we left Marua in the night. . . Look, there is the canoe we came in." He pointed to the dinghy hauled up on the beach.

"O he! Taori!" It was Katafa's voice hailing them from the shore, glad, sweet, clear as a bell, yet far-carrying as the voice of a gull.

As Dick sprang out on the sands he seized her in his arms; parted only a few hours, it seemed to them that they had been weeks apart.

In the old days, even before he was born, his mother Emmeline had never been at ease when separated from his father even by the breadth of the lagoon, the demon that hints of mischance seemed always at her ear.

Dick seemed to have inherited with his power of love for Katafa, something of the dread of mischance for the beloved.

He embraced her, heedless of onlookers, though the only eyes to see were the eyes of the children and of Aioma who had eyes for nothing but the dinghy.

As soon as his foot touched sand, the canoe-builder made for it running like a boy, clapped his hand on the gunnel and then ran it over the planking.

The boats of the Spanish ship of long ago had been clinker-built and had been destroyed in the fight, but he had seen bits of them washed ashore on the southern beach. The dinghy was carvel-built and entire, a perfect specimen of eastern boat-building over which the canoe designer brooded forgetful of Dick and Katafa, the beach he stood on and the sun that lit it.

The idea of a boat built of planking and not hollowed out of a tree trunk had been presented to him by the charred and shattered fragments of the Spanish boats, but how to get planking and how to bend it to the form he desired was beyond his imagination and beyond his means. He saw vaguely that these boats of the papalagi were made somewhat after the fashion of a man, with a backbone and ribs and a covering for the ribs, he saw that by this means enough beam could be obtained to enable the builder to dispense with the outrigger—but then speed, where was there sign of speed in this thing squat and ugly?

In the early ages of the world in which Aioma still dwelt, ugliness had only two expressions, the lines that indicated want of speed and the lines that indicated want of strength.

Dick, though brown as the canoe-builder and almost to be mistaken for a true islander, was perhaps a million years younger than Aioma, just as the dinghy was a million years younger than the fishing canoe that had just brought him across the lagoon. In Dick, Aioma saw the lines that indicated speed and strength, nothing more—he was blind to the nobility of type expressed by that daring face, to the far sight of the eyes and the breadth of the brow; in the dinghy Aioma saw want of speed—he was blind to the nobility of type that made this bud the sister of a battleship, made it a vertebrate as against the dugout which has neither keel nor ribs.

Then Aioma, standing in the sun, a plain canoe-builder and workman in the sight of God and a critic as every true workman is, began to deride the dinghy, at first with chuckles deep down in his throat, then with a sound like the clacking of a hen, then with laughter long and loud and words of derision.

"Which end is which of this pig fish?" inquired Aioma of heaven and Dick, "and he who made her, how many more did he make like her?"

Dick, who had always connected the dinghy with Kearney, and who had a sort of faith that Kearney had made her just as he had made the little model ships, winced at the laughter of the old man. Perhaps it was the white man in him revolting at the derision of a savage over the works of the white man. However that may be, he turned and ran up the beach to the house of Uta Matu which he and Katafa had made their own. There in the shadow, on a hastily constructed shelf stood the little model ships he had so carefully salved from Palm Tree: the frigate, the schooner, the full-rigged ship and the whale man, the last thread connecting him with civilization; toys of the long ago, but no longer toys—fetiches from a world whose very language he had lost, a world of sun and tall trees where like a ghost in the sun dazzle moved a memory that was once a man—Kearney.

He took the schooner from its rest and coming out with it, ran to a great pool in the coral, calling Aioma to come and see what he who made the dinghy had also made.

The pool thirty feet long by twenty broad was ruffled by the breeze from the sea, it was clear as crystal, coral floored—and a trapped school of tiny fish no larger than needles, passed like a silver cloud here and there. Dick on his knees launched the schooner and Aioma standing bent with a hand on each knee watched her as she floated on an even keel. Then on the merry west wind with helm properly set and main boom guyed out she went sailing down the pool to the east where Katafa had run to receive her.

Aioma watched, then Dick running to the other end showed him how she could sail almost against the wind. Dick knew every stick and

HENRY DE VERE STACPOOLE

string of her, how to hoist and lower main and fore and how to set the head sails,—had you placed him on a real schooner, he could have worked her from his knowledge of the model, and Aioma watched vastly intrigued; then, taking a hand, he got on his knees and the great sun saw the builders of the future fleet of Karolin playing like children, whilst the little schooner on its imitation sea sailed from port to port, bowing to the ripples of the pool as the lost *Raratonga,* of which it was the model, had bowed to the swell of the great Pacific.

IV

THE GATES OF MORNING

The break on the reef of Karolin faced due east. Like a harbour mouth it stood, the only entrance to the lagoon, and through it at ebb and flood the sea raced dancing round the coral piers, pouring in and out swift as a river in spate.

When the sun rose he looked straight through the break, and the river of gold from him came level across the dancing waves of the outer sea, rose at the break, as a river rises to flood the coral piers and palms, passed through and spread on the quiet waters of the lagoon.

Mayay amyana—(the way—or the gates—of morning). Ages ago the name had been given to the break and the people who gave it were not speaking in the language of poetry, but of truth, for the one great thing that entered these gates was not the moon, now shrivelled, now full, now absent; nor the tides that altered in time and size; but the morning, eternal, changeless and triumphant.

This great sea gate was more to the people of Karolin than a way of ingress and outgoing; it had a significance deep, almost religious, and based on the experiences of a thousand years, for it was the way to an outer world of which they knew little or nothing, and through it came not only the tides of the sea and the first light of the sun, but also whatever they knew or had known of the world beyond.

The Spanish ship had come in, strange beyond belief, and canoes from the Paumotus had brought war through it—trouble came through the gates of morning no less than joy, and all the dead who had died at sea had passed through them never to return.

To Le Moan just as to Aioma and the others, the sea gate of Karolin was a way and a mystery, a road, yet almost a temple.

But through the gates of morning came other things than ships and men.

Sometimes on a dead calm night and generally at full of moon Karolin lagoon would wake to the sound of thunder, thunder shaking the coral and rolling back in echoes from the far reef, not the thunder of nature, but the thunder of big guns as though fleets were at war on the outer sea.

Then if you came out on the beach you would see the shells bursting in the lagoon, columns of spray rising ghostlike and dissolving in the moonlight whilst the gulls, absolutely indifferent and roosting, stirred never a feather, and the pirate crabs, white as ivory, stood like carved things or went on their business undisturbed.

Natives waking from their sleep, if they woke at all, would turn on the other side and close their eyes again. It was only the *Matura.*

Whip rays twenty feet broad and four feet thick, a school of them at play, flinging themselves ten feet in the air and falling back in a litter of foam and with a concussion striking the lagoon floor and the reef; circling, pursuing one another in their monstrous play, they would keep the echoes rolling beneath the stars, till, as if at a given signal, silence would fall and the great fleet put out to sea again bound for where no man could know.

Awakened from sleep one night, Dick came out on the beach with Katafa. Used to the *Matura* from childhood, she knew and told him, and standing there beside her he had to believe that all this thunder and disturbance was caused by fish.

It was his first real initiation into the wonders of Karolin and the possibilities of the lagoon water. Then, as time went on, in the intervals of the tree-felling, a business in which nearly all the women and boys took part, he would put out by himself to explore the depths and shallows of this great lake that was yet a sea in itself.

On the mind of Dick, almost unstained by the touch of civilization, yet vigorous and developed owing to his civilized ancestry, the world of Karolin exercised a fascination impossible to describe.

Sight, that bird of the soul, could roam here unchecked through the vast distances of sky or rest on a coral branch in the emerald shallows of sea, pursue the frigate mackerel in its rush or the frigate bird in its flight. Out on the lagoon he would crouch sometimes with the paddle across his knees, drifting, idle, without connected thought, environment pressing in upon him till his mind became part of the brilliancy of sea and sky, of the current drift and the wind that blew.

All to the west of a line drawn from mid-reef to mid-reef lay oyster beds, acres in extent and separated by great streaks of hard sand where the fish cast black shadows as they swam, and the crabs scuttered away from the drifting shadow of the canoe; near the northern beach, in ten-fathom water lay the Spanish ship of long ago, coral crusted, with the sea fans waving in the green and the mullet flitting in the shadow of her stern, a thing almost formless, yet with a trace of man's handiwork despite all the work of the coral builders, and still as death in a world where everything was adrift and moving, from the fish sharks that lurked in her shadows to the fucus blown as if by some submarine wind. But the strangest thing in this world of water was the circular current which the outflowing and incoming tides established in its centre, a lazy drift of not more than two knots which was yet sufficient to trap any floating thing and keep it prisoner till a storm broke the spell.

One day Dick ventured so far out that he lost sight of land. Sure of his sense of direction this did not trouble him; he kept on allured by clumps and masses of focus torn loose by the last storm, and drifting with the current, weed alive with sea creatures, tiny crabs, ribbon fish and starry sea-growths brilliant with colour.

Then he put back. But an hour's paddling did not raise the reef; the current was just sufficient to turn the nose of the canoe and he was moving in that fatal circle in which all blind things and things without sense of direction move.

It was noon and the position of the sun gave him no help; sunset or starlight would have put him all right but he had not to wait for these. Then away off beyond a great patch of floating kelp and on his port bow he suddenly saw a dark spot in the sea dazzle. It was a canoe.

Le Moan, as fearless as himself and with a far greater knowledge of these waters, had been fishing along the bank that ran like a spar from the southern beach straight out, shoaling the lagoon water to four fathoms and at some places three. The Karaka bank it was called, and in great storms the lagoon waves broke on it and it showed like a pillow of snow. In ordinary weather nothing marked it but a slight change of colour in the water indicating want of depth.

Away beyond the spur of the Karaka bank, Le Moan saw a canoe adrift and put towards it, guessing from its position and the fact that the paddle was not at work that it was in the grip of the central current.

As she drew near she saw that the canoe man was Taori. She hailed him and he told her that he had lost direction, then, telling him to follow, she put her canoe about and struck the water with the paddle. Though from the elevation of a canoe the horizon showed nothing of the girding reef, her instinct for direction told her exactly how they lay with regard to all the reef points. The marvellous compass in her brain that never failed, and could have steered a ship on the high seas as well as a canoe in Karolin lagoon, told her that the village on the north beach lay over there, and over there her home on the south beach, that the matamata trees lay in such a position and the great palm clump just there.

But as she steered she made not for the north beach where Dick had launched forth and where he lived, but for the south beach where her own home was situated. She said no word but steered, and presently Dick following her saw across the narrowing lagoon the far off Jackfruit trees showing across the water. He knew them and that this was the south beach and anxious to get back to Katafa, he would have turned and made for the northern village where trees were also vaguely, visible, but he felt tired, the paddle was heavy in his hands—he wanted food and he was being led.

Just as the circular current of the lagoon had been sufficient to steer the canoe into a circular course, so was the leading of Le Moan sufficient to bring him to the south beach. A canoe was lying on the south beach and as Dick drew nearer he saw Palia and Tafuta, the two old men companions of Aioma and fellow craftsmen in the art of canoe building.

They were standing by the canoe, in which a woman was seated, and behind them stood the last habitable houses of the village, and behind the houses three coconut trees, hard against the dazzling pale blue of a sky that swept up to burning cobalt. Not a soul was to be seen on all that beach but the two old men.

Then came Le Moan's voice as she hailed them. "O he, Palia, where are the people, and what are you doing with that canoe?"

And Palia's voice answering.

"The word came after you put out this morning calling us to the northern beach for the building. We go. The rest have gone already in the big canoe that brought the word."

Dick at once knew. Aioma yesterday had declared the work far enough advanced to call in all hands including Palia and Tafuta, and the remaining people of the southern tribe.

"Then go," came Le Moan's voice as her canoe stranded on the shelving sand, "but leave me those things and a knife." She went to the canoe and took out some matting, a basket made of coconut sennit and a knife; as Dick brought his canoe ashore Palia and the others were putting off.

"You will follow us?" cried Palia as the paddles struck the water.

"Sometime," replied Le Moan. She turned and began to build a fire to cook the fish she had caught and a breadfruit. Dick, seated on the sand with his knees up and his eyes following the far-off canoe, scarcely noticed her. She was one of the island girls, and though different from the others, of no account to him. An ordinary man would have been struck by her beauty, by her grace, and the fact that she was different from the others, but Katafa had blinded him to other women; it was as though she had put a charm round him, a ring rendering him inviolate to all female approach.

Le Moan, building the fire and preparing the fish and putting the breadfruit to bake, never glanced at him. He was there. The being who had in some extraordinary way suddenly become part of her life was there. This was no ordinary passion of a girl for a man, but something far more recondite and rare; perhaps something half evolved from the yearning of the civilization hidden in her for the civilization in him, perhaps the recognition of race, and that he and she were apart from the island people, those animals man and woman shaped, but destitute of the something that moved like a flame in her mind, lighting nothing—till now.

He was hers just as the sun was hers.

In this first dawn of a love that was to consume her being, she would have died rather than tell him by glance or word the something that filled her mind.

The smoke of the little cooking fire went up like the smoke of an altar.

Who knows but perhaps woman cooking for man was the first priest, the camp fire the first altar, man the first god, his food—the first burnt offering.

An hour later Dick fed, and rested, was pushing his canoe into the water helped by his worshipper.

Then she got into her canoe and accompanied him till the northern beach showed clear before them, the village, and to right of the village the great clump of matamatas, less by three than on the day she had sighted them last.

Here they parted company with the wave of a paddle, Le Moan returning to the desolation of the southern beach, Dick not knowing and not caring whither she went.

HENRY DE VERE STACPOOLE

V

Civilization Peeps in

Without looking back, she turned the nose of her canoe straight for the southern beach. To left of her as she paddled lay the sea gate where the tide was flooding round the coral and the breeze blowing the gulls like snowflakes against the blue; to right the limitless expanse of the lagoon; ahead the desolate beach, the ruined village and the wild tangle of pandanus trees, their limbs wide-spreading as the limbs of an elm, their fronds tossing like ill-kempt hair.

She hauled the light canoe above tide mark, then, turning to the right along the sands, she passed the trees and climbed the coral, standing for a moment facing the south and the empty sea. Then, turning, she gazed across the lagoon to where the far-away northern beach showed its trees above the water dazzle.

It was near full flood and the lagoon was brimming, the outer sea coming in great sheets of smoky blue, whirls of amethyst and streaks of cobalt between the piers of the break. Le Moan could hear the suck of the water through the gates as distinct from the sound of the breakers on the coral, beyond the sound of the breakers the voices of the gulls, beyond the gulls the silence reaching to the white trade clouds on the rim of the purple sea.

She was alone, but for the matter of that, she had always been alone, Aioma and the two old men and the women and children who formed the last remnant of the southern tribe had never been her companions; she had fished with them and helped in the cooking and mat-making, talked with them, lived with them, yet in a way, dwelt apart.

It was the race difference, perhaps, or some bent of soul owing to the fusion of races in her that made her a being quite alone, relying on no one but herself—a creature apart, almost a spirit. She had the power to lose herself utterly when gazing down into clear water as on the day when Dick first saw her gazing into the pond by the trees. Great distances held her in the same way should she give herself over to them, and that strange flair for direction which she shared with the gulls was less perhaps instinctive than psychic, for the mind of Le Moan, eternally in touch with the wind, the sea, the sun and the stars, was clairvoyant to the coming of storm and the sea changes that brought the great tiger sharks into the lagoon, altered the course of the mullet or drove the palu far from the fishing banks to northward of the reef.

Having stood for a while gazing to the north, she came back towards the deserted houses and began to prepare herself some food; after that there were lines to be mended and oap to be cleared from the paraka patch and then came sunset and then the stars, and sleep deeper than the great depths beyond the palu bank.

Had Le Moan looked back across her past, she would have seen a succession of days coloured like the day just dead, brilliancy stretching away into years and opalled by rainy seasons and storms, nights when dreams were unhaunted by human form till tonight, when, towards dawn, a ghostly canoe man showed in the mirror of sleep paddling towards her across a shimmering lagoon.

Then as the dream broke up and the vision vanished, Le Moan awoke beneath the last of the stars, awoke suddenly with fear clutching at her heart and with eyes wide but still half-blinded with sleep.

She sat up. The dawn was breaking and the fishing gulls were putting out to sea; she could hear their voices through the sound of the breakers on the reef. Nothing more, yet she listened, listened with her eyes fixed on the great fan of light showing in the eastern sky against which the gulls showed like withered leaves tossed on the wind.

Nothing. The sea breeze stirred the leaves of the bread-fruit and the branches of the pandamus palms and then fell flat, died out and changed to the first stirring of a land breeze, the highest flying gulls took colour and the ghostly lagoon took form.

The girl rising to her feet swept the lagoon water with her eyes. Nothing. Then, turning, she passed between the trees to the coral of the outer beach and there, out on the ghostly sea and touched by the light of dawn, she saw a ship.

Years after the destruction of the Spanish ship, which had happened before her birth, a whale man had put into the lagoon, cut wood, taken on water, been attacked by Uta Matu, the chief of Karolin, and escaped to the outer sea by a miracle.

Uta would have sent her to the bottom of the lagoon after the Spaniard, for in the depth of his ignorant but instinctive heart lay the knowledge that the black man's burden is the white man and that civilization to the savage means death.

Le Moan could still see as in a glass darkly the fight and the escape of the whale man, and here again was a ship, different in shape from the one of long ago, but arousing in her mind, from association, an instinct of antagonism and dread.

The ship, which had been standing off and on all night, was a schooner, and now as the great sun heaved himself higher and golden ripples broke the sea line, Le Moan watched her take fire, sail after sail catching the light till on the newborn blue of the sea a golden ship lay heaving to the swell, flown round by golden gulls, whose voices came chanting against the breeze like the voices of ghostly sailormen hauling in chorus.

Then as she altered her helm and the wind shivered out of her canvas, a boat was dropped, it ran up a sail and Le Moan, her eyes shaded against the risen sun, saw the boat heading for the break. She ran back amongst the trees and stood for a moment, her hand pressed against her forehead, her mind in confusion, with one idea only fixed and steadfast—Taori.

Here was danger, recollection backed instinct, the powerful instinct of a mind that could tell the north from the south without star or compass, the coming changes of weather, the movement of the fish shoals—the instinct that had awakened her with fear clutching at her heart.

Here was danger to Taori, and now as she stood her hand clasped on her forehead, came the recollection, not only of Uta Matu's fight against the whale man, but of Taori's words to Aioma about the bad men on Marua and the necessity of building the war canoes and of how the young men of Karolin would soon be ripe for war.

But the canoes were not built and the warriors were not ready, and here, suddenly from out of nowhere, had come this great canoe with sails spreading to the sky. Uta Matu and his warriors and fleet were vanished and Taori was unprepared. Then came the thought that the boat making for the break was like the pilot fish that scouts ahead of the tiger shark, it would come into the lagoon and if it found food worth devouring, the tiger shark would follow.

The village on the northern beach was invisible from the break, owing to the trees and the crafty way Uta Matu had set it amongst the trees. She remembered that.

Then her heart suddenly took flame. She would save Taori.

She left the trees and, taking the sand of the inner beach, she began running towards the break. She would attract the boat to her.

You have seen a bird attracting a man away from its nest, heedless of its own fate, thinking only of the thing it loved; just so Le Moan, facing the unknown, which was more terrible than the terrible, sought now to save the being she loved with the love that casts out fear.

She had not run a hundred yards when the boat entered the lagoon, heeling to the breeze and carried by the first of the flood, she flung up her arms to it, then she stood watching as it changed its course making straight towards her.

It was an ordinary ship's quarter boat, painted white, fitted with a mast and lug sail, and Le Moan as she stood watching paralysed and waiting for her fate, saw that she held four men, three kanakas, whose naked shoulders showed above the gunnel, and a huge man, black bearded and wearing a broad-brimmed white straw hat beneath which his face showed dark and terrible as the face of the King of Terrors.

He wore a shirt open at the throat and his shirt sleeves were rolled up showing arms white yet covered with black hair. As the boat grounded and the kanakas sprang out Le Moan scarcely saw them; her eyes were fixed on the great man now standing on the beach, Colin Peterson, no less, one of the last of the sandalwood traders, master and owner of the *Kermadec*—Black Peterson, terrible to look at, swift to strike when roused, yet a man with kindness in his heart and straightness in his soul.

Poor Le Moan, had she only known!

Peterson, sweeping his eyes over the empty and ruined houses and the desolate beach, fixed them on the girl, spoke to her in a tongue she did not understand and then called out:

"Sru!"

A kanaka stepped forward. He was a Paumotuan, a yellow man, and half Malanesian, fierce of face, frizzy headed and wearing a necklace of little shells. After a word with Peterson, he turned to Le Moan and spoke to her and she understood. The language of Karolin was the language of the Paumotas; those far-off islands in the distant days had raided and fought with Karolin, in days still further removed the first inhabitants of Karolin had drifted from the Paumotas but neither Le Moan nor Sru knew aught of this nor of the common ancestry which gave them power of speech.

"I am here alone," said Le Moan answering Sru. "My people are gone—a storm took them all. There is no one here." As she spoke her eyes left Sru and wandered northward to the far trace of the northern beach, the dread at her heart was lest Taori might, by some ill-chance, put out fishing, show himself and be lost, but nothing appeared, nothing but the far-distant trees above the sun blaze on the water.

She knew that the schooner was too far off and too much sheltered by the southern reef for the people on the north beach to see her, that Taori would be busy with the canoe building, yet the dread at her heart drove her to repeat the words automatically like a parrot. "There is no one here but me—my people are gone; a storm took them—I am here alone." As she spoke, she watched Peterson with side glances. She had never seen a bearded man before, and this man with the black curling hair reaching almost to his eyes seemed a monster.

Whilst she was speaking, the other kanakas taking two large water breakers from the boat began to fill them at the well, the well into which she had been looking on the day on which she had first seen Taori.

Colin Peterson stood looking at them, he had half turned from Le Moan and seemed to have forgotten her existence; then, shading his eyes, he looked across and about the lagoon, but he was thinking neither of the kanakas nor the lagoon. He was cursing Le Moan.

He had no use for this girl. He had come ashore for water at this uncharted island thinking maybe to find natives, never dreaming that he would be faced by a problem like this. It was impossible to leave the forlorn creature to her fate, yet what was he to do with her on board of the *Kermadec?* Had it been a man or a boy the matter would have been simple enough, but a girl? If he took her off he would have to find her a home somewhere among the kanakas on one of the northern islands. He was bound for Amao but he reckoned that place was of no use—the kanakas were a bad lot.

As he stood like this thinking and staring about her, Le Moan still watched him, this terrific man who seemed searching with his eyes for Taori.

Would he believe her story—would he kill her? Old tales of the terrible *papalagi* chased through her mind like bats in the dusk that had fallen upon her powers of thought—she did not know. She only knew that she did not care whether he killed her or not as long as he believed her story and departed without hurting Taori.

Then, suddenly, the last breaker of water in the boat, Peterson turned on Sru and shouted to him to fetch her on board. Perplexity in Peterson generally expressed itself in blasphemy, and when Big Feller Mass'r Peterson began to talk like that, Sru never waited for the toe of the boot that was sure to follow.

He seized Le Moan by the arm and pushed her to the boat; for a moment she resisted, then she gave up, tumbled in and squatting forward of the mast saw as one sees in a dream the straining shoulders and tense arms of the kanakas, as, bending and clutching the port and starboard gunnels, they ran the boat out; she saw them tumble on board, felt the grating of the sand and then the balloon-like lift of the waterborne keel; she saw the sail above her take the wind and bulge hard against the blue of the sky; she saw the flying gulls and the wheeling lagoon and the trees of the southern beach vanishing to starboard as the boat headed for the break, but always and above everything she saw the massive hand of Peterson as he sat in the stern sheets with the tiller in the crook of his elbow and his eyes fixed towards her and beyond.

Ai, the sea! What tragedies has it not been partner in? The sea of storms, the blue laughing sea, the sea that now, lovely in the light of morning was flooding gently with the first of the flood through the gates of Karolin, lifting the boat to the outer swell as it passed the coral piers where the gulls cried above the foam of the breakers and the breakers answered to the crying gulls.

If Peterson had killed Le Moan on the beach, she would have met her death without flinching. Seated now watching Karolin drop astern, her eyes never wavered nor softened—even her fear of Peterson had vanished. It was as though she had died on passing the gates of the great atoll and entered a land where personality was not, only perception. A land of pictures that had no relationship to herself or anything she had ever known. She saw as they came alongside the white painted side of the *Kermadec* with the ladder cast down, the rail, and above the rail the great white sail spaces all a-shiver in the wind. The faces of men looking down at the boat, the face of Rantan the mate, and Carlin, a beachcomber picked up at Soma and working his passage north.

Then she was on the deck, which seemed to her broad and white as a beach, and the extraordinary newness of this strange place took on a cutting edge which pierced the deadness that had fallen upon her—this place so vast to her mind that it seemed land of a sort. A moment before, in the boat, the sea had been around her, but here the sea was nothing, this place was everything. Taori, Karolin, the reef, the ocean itself, all for a moment vanished, consumed by the *Kermadec* as by a flame.

And not a soul took notice of her after the first few words of Peterson to the Mate. They were busy getting in the boat and now as the rumbling and threshing of the canvas above died out and the sails filled hard against the blue came the voices of gulls, gulls from the reef and deep-sea gulls flitting in the wake of the *Kermadec* that was now under way.

Le Moan, feeling herself unnoticed, and moving cautiously, came to the weather rail. She saw the reef and the distant trees of Karolin and the following gulls now flying north and south as if giving up the chase. Then the reef line passed from sight beneath the sea dazzle and the voice of the reef and the crying of the gulls died far off, whilst the tree-tops vainly fought with the ever-growing distance, now clinging to the sight, now washed utterly away.

VI

The Men of the *Kermadec*

Now on board that ship there were three men set there by circumstance as pawns in a game of which Taori was king, Katafa queen, and Le Moan perhaps the hand of the player, and these men were Rantan the mate, Carlin the beachcomber, and Sru, bo'sun and chief of the kanakas.

Rantan, a narrow slip of a man, hard bitten and brown as a hickory nut, was a mystery. Perfect in the art of handling a schooner, he knew next to nothing of navigation. Peterson had picked him up as an extra hand and, the mate dying of fever, Rantan had taken his place, making up in general efficiency for his want of higher knowledge. He had spent all his life amongst the islands and natives, he could talk to Sru in his own tongue like a brother born, could pick up the dialect of any island in a week, but had little to say in English. A silent man who never drank, never smoked and never cursed.

Peterson disliked him for no apparent reason whatsoever; he could have got rid of him, but he didn't. Sobriety is a jewel in the Pacific, especially when it is worn by schooner mates.

Carlin had come on board the ship just before she sailed from Soma. He was a big red-headed man useless for anything but beachcombing, he wanted to get up to "them Northern islands" and Peterson out of the heart kindness that had made him take Le Moan on board, took him. He made him work, yet gave him a bunk aft, thus constituting him in a way one of the ship's officers.

Carlin was one of the unfortunates born with a thirst, but in his case it only broke out on land, on board ship he had no wish for liquor but the beach felled him as if with a pole-ax.

Sru, the last of the three men, stood over six feet, stark naked except for a gee-string. He was a man from the beginning of the world. He could cast a spear and find his mark at fifty yards, his nose was flattened, his cheek-bones broad and his face, especially when his eyes were accommodated for distance, wore an expression of ferocity that yet had nothing evil in it. Le Moan had no fear of him. Indeed at the end of her second day on the schooner, she had no fear of anyone on board.

Instinct told her that whatever these men might have done to Taori and the tribe, they would not hurt her. Fortunately she never recognized how utterly useless had been her sacrifice, never recognized the fact that Colin Peterson, so far from hurting Dick, would have been his friend—otherwise she might have cast herself overboard, for her sorrow was heavy on her and wanted no extra weight.

Peterson had given her over to Sru to look after and Sru had made her a shake-down in the long boat. She fed with the kanaka crew, who took their meals on deck, and became part of their family and tribe, but she would not go into the foc'sle, nor would she go into the cabin; those holes in the deck leading down below were, for her, mysterious and terrific; she had peeped down the saloon hatchway and seen the steps going down as into a well and the polish of the handrail and a light below shining on a mat. It was light reflected from the saloon, yet none the less mysterious for that and the whole thing struck her with the enchantment that quite commonplace things sometimes possess for little children, but it was an enchantment tinged with the shadow of dread.

She had no fear of the men on board yet she had a dread of the saloon companionway, of the main boom, till it explained itself to her, of the windlass with its iron teeth. The men, in spite of their clothes and strange ways, shook down as human beings, but the wheel that steered the schooner and the binnacle into which the steersman gazed as he stood moving the spokes, forever moving the spokes of the mysterious wheel, those things were mysterious and their mystery was tinged with the shadow of dread. They were part of the unknown that surrounded her: to the savage the thing unknown is a thing to be feared.

One day when Sru was at the wheel and the deck was empty, she ventured to peep into the binnacle and saw beneath the glittering glass like a star-fish in a rock pool the compass cord trembling like a living thing. Had not the deck been empty so that she dared to speak to Sru on this matter and had not he been in a mood to answer her, the whole life of Le Moan would have been altered and never again might she have seen Taori.

"What is it," asked she, glancing across her shoulder at the steersman, "and why do you look at it so?"

"This," said Sru, indicating the wheel for which he had no word in the native, "moves the steering paddle (*e caya madyara*) and into that I look to find my way."

Now when Karolin had sunk beneath the sea rim the conviction had come to Le Moan that never would she see Karolin again; her instinct told her where it lay and, given a canoe, she could have found it even at this great distance, but her knowledge of where it lay was no comfort to her—she felt that the great hand that had seized her would never let her go and that a door had closed forever between this new world and the old where Taori dwelt safe owing to the closing of the door.

She glanced again at the binnacle and then speaking like a person in reverie she said: "Without that I could find my way though the sea were dark and no stars shone, as I have found my way often in the fishing canoes when the land was so far it could not be seen."

Sru knew what she meant; at Soma in the Paumotus from where he had come the directional instinct, shared more or less by all savages, was especially marked in some of the children, and the deep-sea canoes in those waters where the currents run in an unaccountable manner and where the trade winds are not, depended on the instinct of the steersman.

He bade her close her eyes and turn and turn. "Where now lies the land we have left?" asked Sru. Without opening her eyes and not knowing east from west or north from south, she pointed aft almost dead south.

Sru laughed. She was right, the mysterious compass in her brain that worked without error or deviation would have pointed to Karolin, though a thousand miles away; then as he spun the wheel having let the *Kermadec* a point or two off her course, Le Moan went forward and he forgot her, but he did not forget what she had told him. It remained in his tenacious mind like a pebble in molasses, hidden, but there till three days later when towards evening, the kanakas were eating their supper on deck, Sru was brought face to face and for the first time in his life with a great idea, an idea that included tobacco not by the stick, but in cases, rum in casks, women, barlow knives, chalk pipes and patent leather boots, also canned salmon and seidlitz powders.

Sru, an old pearler, had been in the last of the pearling at Soma before the banks gave out. He knew the value of pearls.

VII

The Pearl

They were seated on the main deck near the galley, their coffee mugs beside them and their plates on their knees and the *Kermadec* on a steady seven-knot clip was heeled slightly to starboard almost rigid as a board, save for the sound of the sea as she dipped to the swell.

For days she had run so with the port rail raised against the white fringe of trade clouds on the far horizon, a steady list from a steady breeze warm and winged with the silver fins of flying fish, a tepid sea-scented wind such as the north can never know, less a wind than a revelation such as men try to express when they speak of the breath of the tropics.

The cook had served out the food, and as they ate he talked; he was a big man with the voice of a child and he was talking of his native village apropos of nothing and to nobody in particular, which is a way kanakas have.

Of the world around them, save for Soma and the southern islands and the island in the north which a few of them knew, Sru, Peroii and the rest of them were as ignorant as Le Moan.

As they talked, the rosy light of sunset falling on them and reflected by the fore canvas, Sru, who was seated by Peroii, saw the wind lift Le Moan's dark hair exposing the pearl charm she wore behind the left ear—the double pearl, lustrous and beautiful, tied in the hair so cunningly and betrayed by the wind.

Le Jennabon had given it to her daughter as a protection against drowning and mischance. More than that it was a love amulet, making sure for the girl a happy married life with a man who would not misuse her. Love amulet or not Le Jennabon had given to her daughter a talisman of extraordinary power. Exposed by the wind for a moment, it had spoken to Sru. It said clearly as tongue could speak, "Karolin is a pearl lagoon." Then as Le Moan raised her hand and tucked the hair back behind her ear, Sru, who had paused in his eating, went on with his food, his dark eyes fixed beyond Peroii, beyond the vision of deck and mast and standing rigging, beyond all things visible, upon wealth: cases of tobacco and rum in many bottles, girls, clay pipes, a gun, and boxes of Swedish matches to strike at pleasure. Karolin lagoon held all these things, the pearl behind Le Moan's ear told him that for a certainty, but Karolin was far astern and he would never see it again, that also was a certainty and before it the heart of Sru became filled with bitterness. A few minutes ago he had been happy and free of care, now his soul was dark as the sea becomes dark with a squall suddenly rising and blowing up out of a clear sky. He had discovered a pearl lagoon—too late. Leaving the others to finish their meal, he rose up and dropped below into the foc'sle, there curled up in his bunk in the gloom he lay to consider this matter.

It was useless to speak of it to Peterson, he would never put the ship back; even if he did he, Sru, would profit little by the matter. He would maybe get a few sticks of tobacco for telling of it, or a knife. Peterson, though kind-hearted enough to rescue Le Moan, was a hard man where bargaining with natives was concerned. Sru had an intimate knowledge of white men, or at least white traders and their ways, and Peterson was a white man to the core.

Then as he lay facing this fact, the idea of Rantan came before him.

Rantan who could talk to him in his own tongue like a brother, who was half a native as far as language and ideas went, and yet was a white man.

Though Rantan had no power to put the ship back, it came into Sru's mind that somehow or in some way this man, clever as all the papalagi were, might be able to do something in the matter. Eased by this idea he turned out of the bunk and came on deck.

The sunset was just vanishing from the sky where in the pansy dusk the constellations were sketching themselves above the vague violet of the sea. Then, suddenly, like the closing of a door, the west went dark and the stars blazed out and bloomed in full sight. The wind, moist, and warm, blew steadily, and Sru, standing in the draught from the head sails, looked about him, forward at the bowsprit rising and falling against the sea stars and aft where the white decks showed, the man at the wheel clearly visible and someone leaning on the weather rail, Carlin to judge by his bulk.

Rantan was nowhere to be seen.

Close to Sru and hunched against some rope coiled by the windlass he saw a figure. It was Le Moan. She was seated with her knees up and her hands round her knees, and she seemed asleep—but she was not asleep, for as Sru's eyes fell on her, her face lifted and he saw the glint of her eyes in the starlight. Those mournful eyes that ever since her departure from Karolin seemed like the eyes of a person in trance, of a dreamer who was yet conscious of some great and real disaster.

Sru instantly forgot Rantan. It seemed that somewhere deep in his shadowy mind something had linked Le Moan with the pearl lagoon and any chance of success in finding it again, raiding it, and turning milk-white chatoyant pearls into sticks of tobacco, bottles of rum, clay pipes and beads to buy love with.

She had given him the indication of what was there, but it seemed to him that she could do more than that.

He crumpled up and sat down beside her on the deck and spoke soft words, asking her what ailed her that she looked so sorrowful. "For," said Sru, "the storm that took your people has without doubt taken many more in the island and will not give them back, not though men weep forever—it is so, and it is so, and ever will be so, and to eat the heart out for that which has been, is to feed foolishly, for," said Sru, "the coral waxes, the palm grows, but man departs." He was repeating the old Island proverb and for a moment he had forgotten Karolin, pearls, gin bottles and the glory of seidlitz powders in effervescence like the foam on the reef; he had forgotten all little things and his words and voice broke up the depths of Le Moan and the cause of her grief came forth. Otherwise and soon she might have died of it. Conscious that Karolin was so far in the past that it was safe to speak, she told Sru that no storm had overtaken her people, that she had lied to Peterson so that he might not discover and perhaps kill the being she loved; and there, sitting in the showering starlight, she did that which she had never done before even for her own inspection, opened her heart, told, as a sleeper might tell in sleep, of her love for Taori and of his beauty and strength and swiftness and of everything except that which she did not know—the fact that Taori had a lover already, Katafa.

She spoke and Sru listened, absorbing her words and her story as a kanaka will absorb any sort of tale he can understand. Then this amazing savage who had spoken so poetically about the waxing of the coral and the passing of man, this sympathizer who had spoken so softly in addressing grief, leaning on his elbow began to shake with laughter.

He knew that big feller Mas'r Peterson would not have hurt a hair of Taori's head, that he did not want to take Le Moan off the beach and had only done so because he imagined her unable to fend for herself. He saw that Le Moan, trying to protect her lover against imaginary perils had allowed herself to be sacrificed and snatched away from everything she loved and cared for, that she had prepared for herself the trap into which she had fallen—and all this to the mind of Sru seemed a huge joke, almost as good as the joke of the drunken man he had once seen, who, trying to cut wood with his foot on a log had cut off his foot with the axe he was wielding.

Sru giggled like a girl being tickled, then he burst out in snorts like a buffalo in a temper, choked as though he had swallowed a fish-bone and then began to explain.

Began to explain and failed to hit the mark simply because Le Moan could not understand why big feller Mas'r Peterson had taken her away from Karolin. He did not want to take her away yet he had taken her away. Le Moan could not understand that in the least.

Le Moan could not understand pity, she had never come across it in others and she had never felt it for herself. Had she been able to pity herself, she would have flung herself on the deck weeping and wailing when the *Kermadec* turned her stern to the south and dropped Karolin beyond the horizon. She had sacrificed herself for the sake of the being who dominated her existence, she had dared the most terrible of all things, the unknown, yet she could not in the least understand why Peterson should do what he did not want to do for the sake of a being, a stranger whom he had never seen before.

To tell the truth Sru did not quite comprehend it either, he knew it was so and he left it at that. It was one of the strange and unaccountable things that white men were always doing. What intrigued him was the fact that Le Moan had fooled herself in fancying Peterson a dangerous man capable of injuring her lover and that Peterson had fooled himself in believing her story.

So he talked till Le Moan at last understood the fact that, whatever Peterson's object in taking her away may have been, he would not have injured Taori, that if she had said nothing he would have gone off after having filled the water breakers at the well, and as he talked and as she listened dumb before the great truth that she had sacrificed everything for nothing, slowly up from the subconscious mind of Sru and urged by his talk, came an idea.

"You will go back," said Sru. "Listen, it is I, Sru, who am talking— we will go back, you and I, and what tells me is that which lies behind thy left ear."

Le Moan put her hand up to the amulet hidden beneath her hair.

HENRY DE VERE STACPOOLE

"We will go back," went on Sru, "you and I and another man, and perhaps more, all good men who will not hurt Taori—but Pete'son, no—no," he murmured as if communing with some dark spirit. "He would swallow all. He alone knows the way across the sea, so that setting the steering paddle this way or that he can go straight as the frigate bird to Soma or to Nalauka or to what island or land he chooses, he alone of the men on board this ship. But thou art wise as he. Wise as the frigate bird that leaves the land far from sight yet can return. You will guide us to Karolin. Can your eyes still see that beach and where it lies?"

Le Moan threw out her arms.

"Though I were blind as the sand worm, I could find it," said Le Moan, "through night and storm—but when?"

"No man can hurry the rising of the day," said Sru, "but soon it will come and soon your eyes shall fall upon Taori—that which lies behind your left ear has told me, and it has told me more. Answer so that I may know if it speak the truth. It has told me that thick in that lagoon lie the shells of the *iyama* (oyster) from whence it came—is that true talk?"

"Thick and far they lie," said Le Moan, "from the *kaaka* far as one can paddle from the coming in to the middle of the tide."

"So," said Sru, "it spoke the truth. When we make our return you will go to meet Taori and we to find the *iyama* for the sake of the stones they hold, brethren of that which lies. . . there."

He touched her hair behind her left ear and rose gliding off aft, whilst Le Moan, whose life had suddenly come back to her, sat gazing through night and beyond the stars at a sunlit beach where spear in hand and lovely as the morning stood Taori.

Taori who at that moment tired out with the labour of canoe-building was lying asleep with his arm across the warm body of Katafa.

VIII

THE MIND OF SRU

N ow the mind of Sru had sat down to talk with Le Moan, having in it no plan—nothing but a desire for pearls and what pearls would bring, and the knowledge sure and instinctive that Karolin was a pearl lagoon. It had risen up armed with a plan.

This plan had come to him from his close contact and talk with Le Moan. Brooding alone with nothing for his mind to cling to, it is doubtful if Sru could have evolved a plan; the presence of the girl, her connection with Karolin, her story, her wish to get back, the fact that she was a pathfinder and the fact that Peterson, even if he took the *Kermadec* back, would take all the profit of the business for himself—all these thoughts and considerations came together in Sru's mind and held together like a cluster of bees, owing to the presence of the girl who was the core and centre of everything. He would speak of the matter to Rantan. Sru understood that Karolin was not on the charts, those mysterious pieces of paper that enabled Peterson to find his way about, he understood that Rantan had little knowledge of navigation, he only knew that were they to steer south for as many days as they had steered north and then hand the steering over to Le Moan, she would bring them to the place desired.

Give her the wheel right away and she would steer them back, but she could not stand at the wheel for days and days; no, it would be enough to steer south by the compass and then when close on the latitude hand the wheel to her. The instinct that led the birds over unmarked sea spaces and the palu from hundreds of miles away to the self-same breeding grounds, that would be sufficient.

Going aft he hung about for a while close to the fellow at the wheel, but there was no sign of Rantan and Peterson coming on deck. Sru went forward again and dropped below to the foc's'le. It was in the morning watch that he found his opportunity, only Rantan and the steersman were aft and Sru coming along, stood with the mate by the rail.

The dawn was full on the sea.

They spoke for a minute on the prospect of the wind holding, and then Sru, with a glance at the steersman to make sure he was out of hearing, came to his subject.

"That land we have left," said Sru, "is Karolin—the girl has told me the name, but much more as well. That lagoon is a pearl lagoon. This is a private matter between us. I tell you because I could not tell anyone else and because I think we may profit by it."

"A pearl lagoon," said Rantan. "Is she speaking the truth?"

"The truth. She wears behind her ear two pearls in one, so," said Sru, joining his closed fists in the dawn light, "they are tied in her hair and the wind lifting her hair I saw them; then I spoke and she told me. Now listen, Ra'tan, we know of this matter, you and I, we two alone will get those pearls—Pete'son, no. He would swallow them all and give us the shells to eat, but how we are to go has not been shown to me, it is for you to see to that matter."

All this he said in the native and Rantan, listening, tapped out the ashes from his pipe against his heel, and then, pipe in hand, leaned against the rail, his eyes fixed on the deck.

In the increasing light he could see the deck planking clearly even to the dowels. Plunged fathoms deep in thought he said nothing for a while, then raising his eyes he spoke.

"What you say is true, but Pete'son is the wisest of us. How can we find that island again without him? As you know, my life has been spent mostly among the islands—shore along and between island and island as they lie in the Paumotas ten to a space as broad as your palm. I can handle this ship or any ship like this or any canoe, as you know, but to look at the sun at noon as Pete'son looks, and to say 'I am here, or here,' that art has not been given me. I have not lived my life on the deep sea, but only in shallow waters. Then again Pete'son is not the full owner of this ship, there is another man who owns a part and without talking to him he cannot break a voyage, he cannot say, I will go here or here without the other man saying yes."

"That is the more reason," said Sru, "that we must go without him."

"And without him we cannot find our way," replied Rantan.

Then Sru told of Le Moan's power of direction finding. Rantan understood at once, he had seen the thing often amongst the natives of Soma and other islands and the fact came suddenly on his mind like the blow of a hammer riveting things together.

But he said nothing to show exactly what was in his mind, he heard Sru out, and told him to go forward and not speak of the matter to anyone. "For," said Rantan, "there may be something in what you say. I do not know yet, but I will think the matter over."

Left alone he stood, his eyes on the sun blaze creeping upon the eastern horizon. He was a quick thinker. The thing was possible, and if Karolin lagoon was a true pearl lagoon the thing was a fortune.

By taking the *Kermadec* there with the kanaka crew for divers, eight months or a year's work would give the profit of twenty voyages. Well he knew that if Colin Peterson were the chief of that expedition, there would be little profit for anyone but Peterson and his partner. Peterson would have to be eliminated if there was any work to be done in this business.

Sru had not said a word about Taori or Le Moan's untruth as to Karolin being uninhabited.

It would have tangled the story for one thing, and for another might not Ra'tan say to himself. "If this girl has lied on one matter, may she not be lying about the pearls?" Sru knew instinctively that she spoke the truth, and he left it at that, and Rantan watching now the glory of the rising sun, stood, his plan crystallizing into full shape, his eyes gazing not on the sunlit sea, but on Karolin, a desolate atoll, uninhabited, with no eyes to watch what might be done there but the eyes of the seagulls.

IX

CASHI

L e Moan had never known pity. She had lived amongst the pitiless, and if any seed of the divine flower lay in her heart it had never grown nor come to blossom. She had seen her tribe raided and destroyed and the remnants chased to sea by the northern tribe under Uta Matu, she had seen battle and murder and sudden death, storm and destruction; she had seen sword-fish at war and the madness and blood-lust of fish, bow-head whales destroyed by orcas and tiger sharks taking men—all these things had left her unmoved by pity as they would have left Rantan. Yet between these two pitiless ones lay a distance greater than that between star and star.

Le Moan had sacrificed herself for the sake of Taori; had faced what was more terrible than death—the unknown, for the sake of the man who had inspired her with passion; and had found what was more terrible than death—separation.

To return and find Taori she would, if necessary, have destroyed the *Kermadec* and her crew without a second thought, just as to save him she would have destroyed herself. Rantan could not have understood this, even if it had been carefully explained to him with diagrams exhibiting the savage soul of Le Moan, all dark, save where at a point it blazed into flame.

All that day working out his black plan he reviewed his instruments, Sru, Carlin, the crew, the ship, and last and least the kanaka girl who would act as a compass and a navigator. A creature of no account save the instinct she shared with the fish and the birds, so he fancied.

The *Kermadec* had loaded some turtle shell at Soma and at Levua she was to pick up a cargo of sandalwood. San Francisco was the next port of call, but to Rantan's mind it did not seem probable that she would ever reach San Francisco. It all depended on Carlin. Rantan could not do the business alone even with the help of Sru; Carlin was a beachcomber and to leave him with a full whiskey bottle would have been fatal for the whiskey bottle, but he was a white man; he would have been fired off any ship but the *Kermadec*, but he was a white man. Rantan felt the necessity of having a white man with him on the desperate venture which he had planned, and taking Carlin aside that night he began to sound him.

"We're due at Levua tomorrow," said Rantan. "Ever been to Levua?"

"Don't know it," replied the other, "don't want to neither; by all accounts, listening to the old man, there's nothing there but one dam' sandalwood trader and the karakas he uses for cutting the wood. I want to beach at Tahiti, that's where I'm nosing for when I get to 'Frisco; there's boats in plenty running down from 'Frisco to Tahiti."

"Maybe," said Rantan, "but seems to me there's not much doing at Tahiti. Hasn't it ever hit you that there's money to be made in the islands and better work to be done than bumming about on the beach? I don't mean hard work, handling cargo or running a ship—I mean money to be picked up, easy money and plenty of it."

The big red man laughed and spat over the rail.

"Not much," said he, "not by the likes of me or you; clam shells is all there's to be picked up by the likes of me and you when the other chaps have eaten the chowder."

"How'd you like ten thousand dollars in your fist?" asked Rantan, "twenty—thirty—there's no knowing what it might come to, and all for no work at all but just watching kanakas diving for pearls."

Carlin glanced sideways at his companion.

"What are you getting at?" asked he.

"Well, I'll tell you," said Rantan, "I know of a pearl island and it's not far from here. It's a sealed lagoon, never been worked, and there's enough there to make a dozen men rich, but to get there I'd want a ship, but I haven't got one nor the money to charter one; I'm like you, see?"

"What are you getting at?" asked Carlin again, a new tone in his voice.

"I'm just saying I haven't a ship," replied the other, "but I know where to get one if I could find a chap to help me in the taking of her."

Carlin leaned further over the rail and spat again into the sea. With terrible instinct he had taken up the full meaning of the other.

"And how about the kanakas?" asked he, "kanakas are dam' fools, but get them into a court of law and they're bilge pumps for turning up the evidence. I've seen it," he finished, wiping his mouth with the back of his hand. "A sinking job it was, and the chap that did it got ten years, on kanaka evidence."

Rantan laughed. "Leave the kanakas to me," said he, "I'm putting it to you—if I've the sand to do the job, would you help?"

HENRY DE VERE STACPOOLE

"I'm not saying I wouldn't," said Carlin, "but what about the navigating? You aren't much good on that job. . . or are you? I'm thinking maybe you've been holding it up your sleeve."

"I'm good enough to get there," replied Rantan. "Well, think it over, we've time in our hands and no need to hurry. But remember there's no knowing the money in the business, and if it comes to doing it, don't you worry about risks; I'm not a man to take more than ordinary risks and I'll fix everything."

Then he turned away and walked aft leaving Carlin leaning on the rail.

Whatever Carlin's start in life may have been, he was now beach-worn like one of the old cans you find tossing about the reef flung away by the kanakas—label gone, and nothing to indicate its past contents. The best men in the world would wilt on the beach, and that's the truth; the beach, that is to say sun and little to do—the sun kills or demoralizes more men than whiskey; to be born to the sun, you must be born in the sun, like Katafa, like Dick, like Le Moan; you must never have worn clothes.

Sometimes a white man is sun proof inside and out, but rarely. Carlin was sun proof on the outside, his skin stood the pelting of the terrible invisible rays; he throve on it; but internally he had gone to pieces.

He had one ambition, whiskey—or rum, or gin, or even samshu, but whiskey for choice.

There was whiskey on the *Kermadec*, but not for Carlin. Peterson, as sober a man as Rantan, kept it, just as he kept the Viterli rifles in the arms rack, for use in an emergency. It was under lock and key, but Carlin had smelt it out.

Its presence on board was like the presence of an evil genius, invisible, but there and exercising its power; it kept reminding him of Rantan's words at supper that night, and when he turned in and even in his sleep its work went on; he saw in his dreams the vessel heading for the unknown pearl island towards the golden light of fortune and unlimited whiskey, he was on her deck with Rantan in command and Peterson was not there.

The dream said nothing about Peterson, totally ignored him, and Peterson, on deck at that moment, had no idea that the beachcomber was dreaming of the *Kermadec* off her course and without her skipper.

Next day in the morning watch, Sru was at the wheel and Rantan, a pipe in his mouth, stood by the weather rail, the sun had just risen shattering the night and spreading gold across the breezed up blue of the swell.

The sunrise came to the *Kermadec* like the sudden clap of a hot hand: Sru felt it on his back and Rantan on his cheek. From away to windward came the cry of a gull, a gull passed overhead with domed wings circled as if inspecting the schooner and drifted off on the wind. Almost at the same moment, came the cry of the kanaka lookout. "Land!"

Rantan walked forward. Right ahead, rosy above the brimming sea, lay the cloud scarf of Levua.

Still a great way off, facing the blazing east, the island, clear of any trace of morning bank, seemed to float between the blue of sea and sky, remote, more lovely than any dream.

When Rantan turned aft again he found Le Moan standing by Sru at the wheel. Sru was explaining to her how the wheel worked the "steering paddle" in the stern. The *Kermadec* was close hauled, every sail drawing, Sru was explaining this matter and showing how the least bit closer to the wind would set the sails shivering and take the way off the ship. Le Moan understood. Sea craft was born in her, and used now to the vast sail spaces of the schooner, she felt no fear—the *Kermadec* was only a canoe after all, of a larger build and different make.

He let her hold the spokes for a moment, governing the wheel with a guiding hand, then at the risk of the schooner being taken aback, he stood aside and the girl had the helm.

The *Kermadec* for a moment showed no sign that the wheel had changed hands, then, suddenly, a little warning flutter passed through the canvas from the luff of the mainsail, passed and ceased and the sail became hard again. Le Moan had understood, understood instinctively, that ceaseless pressure against the lee bow which tends to push a vessel's head up into the wind.

For a moment Taori, Karolin, the very presence of Sru were forgotten, the words that Sru had spoken to her only a little while before, "You will soon see Taori, little one, but first you must learn to use the steering paddle." Everything was forgotten in the first new grip of the power that was in her to hold all those great sail spaces filling, to play such a great game with the wind and the sea.

Aioma had taught her to steer her fishing canoe, but so long ago that she could not remember the first time she had the paddle to herself; but this was different, different as the kiss of a lover from the kiss of a friend—something that reached her soul; it was different as the sight of Taori from the sight of other men, great, thrilling, lifting her above herself, creative.

Utterly ignorant of the mechanism that moved the rudder as a man is ignorant of the mechanism that moves his arm, after the first few minutes of the great new experience she could not do wrong. She knew nothing of the compass, she only knew that she was to keep the ship close hauled as Sru had been keeping her, so close that a fraction nearer the wind would spill the sails. Sru watched her and Rantan, forgetting his pipe, stood with his eyes fixed on her. Both men recognized that the ship was safe for the moment. One might have thought them admiring the picture that she made against the blue sky and the glory of morning, but the interest in their eyes was neither the interest of the roused æsthetic sense, nor of love, nor of passion, nor of seamanship.

As they stood, suddenly, and as though Tragedy had staged the scene for some viewless audience, the head and shoulders of Peterson appeared at the saloon hatch opening.

Rantan, his face mottled with white, stared at Peterson, Sru drawing the back of his hand across his nose as if wiping it, stood on one foot, then on the other, confused, looking like a dog that has been misbehaving itself. Le Moan saw nothing.

Without losing its alertness on the touch of the wheel her mind had gone off for a momentary flight. She saw herself steering the *Kermadec* towards Karolin, she saw in imagination the distant reef, the gulls and the thrilling blue of the great lagoon beyond the reef opening.

Peterson, without coming further on deck, watched her for a moment without comprehending anything but the fact that the girl had been allowed to take the wheel. Then as Sru took the spokes from her and pushed her forward, the captain of the *Kermadec* turned on Rantan, but the abuse on his lips was half shrivelled by the face of the mate.

"Don't you never do a thing like that again," said Peterson. "Dam' tomfoolery." He snorted and went forward, kicked a kanaka out of his way and then stood, his eyes fixed on the distant vision of Levua opal tinted in the blue, blue north.

X

The High Island

They came in on a dying wind, the outlying reefs creaming to the swell and the great high island opening its cañons and mountain glades as they drew towards it pursued by the chanting gulls.

Le Moan, who had never seen a high island or only the vision of Palm Tree uplifted by mirage, stood with her eyes fixed on the multitude of the trees. Palms, breadfruit, tree ferns, aoas, sandalwood groves, trees mounting towards the skies, reaching ever upwards, changing in form and misted by the smoke of torrents.

Here there was no freedom, the great spaces of the sea had vanished, Levua like an ogre had seized her mind and made it a prisoner.

For the first time in her life something came to her heart, terrible as her grief for the loss of Taori, yet even more far searching and taking its bitterness from the remote past as well as the present. It was the homesickness of the atoll-bred islander encompassed by the new world of the high island; of the caged gull taken from the freedom of the wind and the sea.

At Karolin you could see the sun from his rising to his setting, and the stars from sea line to sea line; the reef rose nowhere to more than twice the height of a man, the sea was a glittering plain of freedom and a sound and a scent.

Worse even than the monstrous height of Levua, its strange cañons and gloomy woods, was the scent of the foliage, cossi and vanilla and sandalwood, unknown flowers, unknown plants, all mixed with the smell of earth and breathing from the glasshouse atmosphere of the groves.

An extraordinary thing was the way in which the forms and perfumes of Levua permeated the *Kermadec* itself, so that, turning her eyes away from the land, the deck of the schooner, the rails, masts and spars, all seemed hostile to her as the land itself. Sru alone gave her comfort as she watched him superintending the fellows busy with the anchor—Sru, who had promised that she would return.

The anchor fell in twelve-fathom water and as the the rumble-tumble of the anchor chain came back in echoes from the moist-throated woods, a boat put out from the beach. It was Sanders the white trader, the man who lived here alone year in, year out, taking toll of the sandalwood trees, paying the natives for their labour in trade goods; cut off from the world, without books, without friends, and with no interest beyond the zone of sea encircling the island, except the interest of his steadily accumulating money in the hands of his agents—the Bank of California.

The face of the white man showed thin and expressionless as a wedge of ice as he came over the rail like a ghost and slipped down to the cabin with Peterson to talk business.

Rantan and Carlin leaned over the side and watched the kanakas in the boat pulling forward to talk to the schooner crew congregated at the rail by the foc'sle head.

The beach lay only a cable length or two away, empty except for a couple of fishing canoes drawn up beyond tide mark; no house was to be seen, the village lying back among the trees, and no sound came from all that incredible wealth of verdure—nothing, but the far voice of a torrent, raving yet slumbrous and mixed with the hush of the surf on the reefs and beach.

"Notice that chap," said Carlin, "didn't look to right or left of him, same's if he'd been doped. Reckon he's full of money too if he's the only trader here—notice his white ducks and his dandy hat and the mug under it? I know the sort. Drink turns to vinegar in a chap like that and that's the sort that makes money in the islands."

"Or the fellows that aren't afraid to put their hands on the stuff when they see it," replied Rantan. "Well, what about that pearl island I was speaking of?"

"And that hooker you were going to take to get there," cut in Carlin. "Put me on her deck and I'm with you."

"You're on it," replied Rantan.

Carlin laughed. He had known Rantan's meaning all along and this strange game of evasion between the two had nothing to do with the *Kermadec*, but with something neither dared to discuss one with the other: Peterson, and what was to be done with Peterson.

"You're on it," continued Rantan, "and now what do you say?"

"I'm with you," replied Carlin, "but I don't see how you're to do it. I'll have no hand in doing it."

"Leave that to me," said the other, "you've only to help work the ship when I've taken her."

"You say Sanders is the only white man here," said Carlin.

"So Peterson tells me," replied Rantan.

"Well, one white man is enough to turn on us," said Carlin.

"He won't turn on us," replied Rantan grimly, and Carlin glancing at him sideways wondered for a moment if he hadn't the devil in tow with Rantan. But Carlin was of the type that will take profit and not care so long as its own hands are clean. I wonder how many of us would eat meat if we had to do the killing ourselves or make money from poisonous industries if we had ourselves to face the poison. What Rantan chose to do was nothing to Carlin so long as he himself had not to do it or to plan it, but he was cautious.

"How about that chap Sru?" he asked. "He's boss of the crew and the only thinking one of them—suppose. . ."

"Nothing," replied the other. "He's with me."

Fell a silence filled with the voice of the far torrent and the murmur of the sea, a hush-a-bye sound through which vaguely came the murmur of voices through the skylight of the saloon where Peterson and the trader were discussing prices and freights, each absorbed by the one sole idea, profit at the expense of the other.

XI

THE TRAGEDY

The Pacific has many industries but none more appealing to the imagination than the old sandalwood trade, a perfumed business that died when copra found its own, before the novelist and the soap boiler came to work the sea of romance, before the B. P. boats churned its swell or Honolulu learned to talk the language of San Francisco.

In those days Levua showed above the billowing green of the breadfruit, the seaward nodding palms, and the tossing fronds of the dracænas, a belt, visible from the sea, where the sandalwood trees grew and flourished. Trees like the myrtle, many branched and not more than a foot thick in the trunk, with a white deliciously perfumed wood deepening to yellow at the root.

Sanders, the trader of Levua who exported this timber, paid for it in trade goods, so many sticks of tobacco at five cents a stick, so many coloured beads or pieces of hoop iron wherewith to make knives, for a tree. He paid this price to Tahuku the chief of the tribe and he paid nothing for the work of tree felling, barking, and cutting the wood into billets. Tahuku arranged all that. He was the capitalist of Levua, though his only capital was his own ferocity and cunning, the trees rightfully belonged to all. The billets already cut and stored in go-downs were rafted across the lagoon in fragment heaps to the *Kermadec* and shot on board from hand to hand, piled on deck and then stowed in the hold, a slow business watched by Le Moan with uncomprehending eyes. She knew nothing of trade. She only knew what Sru had promised her, that soon, very soon, the ship would turn and go south to find Karolin once again. She believed him because he spoke the truth and she had an instinct for the truth keen as her instinct for direction, so she waited and watched whilst the cargo came leisurely and day by day and week by week, the cargo bound for nowhere, never to be sold, never to be turned into incense, beads, fancy boxes and cabinets; the cargo only submitted to by the powers that had taken command of the *Kermadec* and her captain, because until the cargo was on board, the ship would not take on her water and her sea-going stores in the shape of bananas and taro.

Down through the paths where the great tree ferns grew on either side and the artu and Jack-fruit trees cast their shadows, came the men of Levua, naked, like polished mahogany, and bearing the white perfumed billets of sandalwood; as they rafted them across the diamond-clear emerald-green water to where the *Kermadec* stood in the sapphire blue of twelve fathoms their songs came and went on the wind, the singers unconscious that all the business of that beach was as futile as the labour of ants or the movement of shadows, made useless by the power of the pearl Le Moan carried behind her left ear.

The night before sailing, the water and fruit were brought on board and Peterson went ashore to have supper with Sanders taking Rantan with him. Carlin remained behind to look after the ship.

It was a lovely evening, the light of sunset rose-gold on the foam of the reefs and gliding the heights of Levua, the trees and the bursting torrent whose far-off voice filled the air with a mist of sound. Carlin, leaning on the rail, watched the boat row ashore, Sru at the stern oar, Peterson steering. He watched Peterson and the mate walk up the beach and disappear amongst the trees; they had evidently given orders that the boat was to wait for them on the beach, for, instead of returning, Sru and his men squatted on the sands, lit their pipes and fell to playing su-ken, tossing pebbles and bits of coral in the air and catching them on the backs of their hands.

Carlin lit his pipe. What he was watching was more interesting than any stage play, for he knew that the hour had struck, that the water and stores were on board and the ship due to raise her anchor at sunrise.

He stood with his eyes fixed on the beach. The trader's house and store lay only a few hundred yards back among the trees and the native village quarter of a mile beyond and close to the beginning of the sandalwood groves; would any trouble in the trader's house be heard by the people of the village? He put this question to himself in a general way and the answer came "No." Not unless shots were fired; but then without shooting—how—how—how?

How what?

He did not enter into details with himself. He stood watching the men on the beach and then he saw Sru as if suddenly tired of the game they were playing, rise up, stretch himself and stroll towards the boat. Near the boat a fishing canoe was beached and Sru having contemplated the boat for a minute or so turned his attention to the canoe. He examined the outrigger, pressed his foot on it and then bending over the interior picked out something—it was a fish spear with a single barb. Carlin remembered that Rantan on landing had looked into the canoe, as though from curiosity or as if to make sure there was something in it. Who could tell?

The fish spear seemed to interest Sru. He poised it as if for a throw, examined the barb and then, spear in hand, came back to the fellows who were still playing their game and sat down. Carlin saw him exhibiting the spear to them, poised it, talking, telling no doubt old stories of fish he had killed on the reef at Soma; then, as if tired, he threw the thing on the sand beside him and lay back whilst the others continued their endless game.

Then came dark and the steadily increasing shower of star-light till the coal sack showed in the milky way like a hole punched in marble and the beach like a beach in ghost-land, the figures on it clearly defined and especially now the figure of Sru, who had suddenly risen as though alarmed and was standing spear in hand.

Then at a run he made for the trees and vanished.

CARLIN TURNED AWAY FROM THE rail and spat. The palms of his hands were sweating and something went knock, knock, knock, in his ears with every beat of his heart. The kanakas on board were down in the foc'sle from which a thin island voice rose singing an endless song, the deck was clear only for the figure of Le Moan—and Carlin, half crazy with excitement, not daring to look towards the beach, walking like a drunken man up and down began to shout and talk to the girl.

"Hi, you kanaka girl," cried Carlin, "something up on the beach— Lord God! she can't talk, why can't you talk, hey? Whacha staring at me dumb for? Rouse the chaps forward, we'll be wantin' the anchor up" . . . He went to the foc'sle head and kicked—calling to the hands below to tumble up, tumble up, and to hell with their singing for there was something going on on the beach. Ruining everything, himself included, if they had been a white crew; then making a dash down to the saloon he beat and smashed at the store cupboard where he knew the whiskey was kept, beat with his naked fists till the panels gave and he tore them out, and breaking the neck of a whiskey bottle, drank with bleeding lips till a quarter of the bottle was gone.

Then he sat at the table still clutching the bottle by the neck but himself again. The nerve crisis had passed suddenly as it had come.

Yes, there was something going on upon the beach that night when, as Le Moan and the crew crowding to the port rail watched, the figure of Rantan suddenly broke from the trees and came running across the sands towards the boat followed by Sru.

She heard the voice of Sru shouting to the boat kanakas: "Tahuku has slain the white man, the trader and Pete'son have been slain." She saw the boat rushed out into the starlit water and as it came along towards the ship, she saw some of the crew rush to the windlass and begin heaving the anchor chain short whilst others fought to get the gaskets off the jib and raise the mainsail. Already alarmed by Carlin the words of Sru completed the business. Tahuku was out for killing and as they laboured and shouted, Carlin hearing the uproar on deck, put the whiskey bottle upstanding in a bunk and came tumbling up the ladder and almost into the arms of Rantan who came tumbling over the rail.

XII

They Make South

Then from the shore you might have seen the *Kermadec* like a frightened bird unfolding her wings as the boat came on board and the anchor came home, mainsail, foresail and jib filling to the steady wind coming like an accomplice out of the west, the forefoot cutting a ripple in the starlit waters of the lagoon and the stern swinging slowly towards Levua, where two white men lay dead in the trader's house and where in the village by the sandal grove Tahuku and his men lay asleep, unconscious of what civilization had done in their name.

Rantan, steering, brought the ship through the broad passage in the reefs where the starlight lit the spray of the breaking swell, the vessel lifting to the heave of the sea caught a stronger flow of wind and with the main boom swung to port headed due south.

Rantan handed the wheel to Sru and turned to a bundle lying in the port scuppers. It was Carlin sound asleep and snoring; the mate touched the beachcomber with his foot and then turning, went below.

He saw the locker smashed open and the whiskey bottle in the bunk, he opened a porthole and flung the bottle out and then turning to the locker, searched it. There were two more bottles in the locker and having sent them after the first, he closed the port and sat down at the table under the swinging lamp.

Kermadec, cargo, crew and ship's money were his; the crew knew nothing except that Tahuku had killed Pete'son and the white trader; there was no man to speak except Sru, who dared not speak, and Carlin who knew nothing definite. In time and at a proper season it was possible that these might be rendered dumb and out of count, and this would be the story of the *Kermadec.*

WITHOUT HER CAPTAIN, MURDERED BY the natives of Levua, and navigated by her mate, who knew little or nothing of navigation, she had attempted to make back to Soma; had missed Soma and found a big lagoon island, Karolin, which was not on the charts. There Sru, the bo'sun, and Carolin, a white man, had died of fish poisoning, and there she had lain for a year—doing what. . . ?

"And what were you doing all that time, Mr. Rantan?" The question was being put to him before an imaginary Admiralty court, and the answer "Pearling" could not be given.

It was only now, with everything done and the ship his, that the final moves in the game were asking to be solved; up to this the first moves had claimed all his mental energy.

The *Kermadec* could be lost on some civilized coast quite easily, everything would be quite easy but the accounting for that infernal year—and it would take a year at least to make good in a pearl lagoon.

No, the *Kermadec* must never come within touch of civilization again, once he was sure of the pearl ground being worth working; the vessel must go; with the longboat he might get at last back to Soma or some of the Paumotuan islands—might.

The fact of his ignorance of navigation that had helped his story so far, hit him now on the other side, the fact so useful before a Board of Trade enquiry would help him little with the winds and tides and to the winds and tides he had committed himself in the long run.

He came on deck. The crew, all but the watch, had crowded down into the foc'sle where all danger over and well at sea, they had turned in. Sru was still at the wheel and Le Moan, who had been talking to him, vanished forward as the mate appeared in the starlight and stood watching for a moment the far-off loom of the land.

Carlin still slept. He had rolled over on his back and was lying, mouth open and one hand stretched out on the deck planking, his snores mixed with the sound of the bow wash and the creaking of the gaff jaws and cordage.

Rantan looked into the binnacle, then with a glance at Carlin he turned to Sru.

The Paumotuan did not speak, he did not seem to see the mate or recognize his presence on deck, the whites of his eyeballs showed in the starlight; and as he steered, true as a hair to the course, his lips kept working as he muttered to himself.

He looked like a man scared, and steering, alone, out of some imminent danger, that appearance of being isolated was the strangest thing. It made Rantan feel for a moment as though he were not there, as though the *Kermadec* were a ship deserted by all but the steersman.

Sru was scared. Steering true as an automaton, his mind was far away in the land of vacancy and pursued by white feller Mas'r Pete'son. It had come on him like a stroke when Le Moan, approaching him, had asked where the bearded man was who had gone ashore and not returned. He had no fear of Le Moan or her question, but out of it Peterson had come, the white man whom he had always feared yet whom he had dared to kill. The appalling power that had strengthened his arm and mind, the power of the vision of tobacco unlimited, Swedish matches, knives, gin and seidlitz powders, was no longer with him—Peterson was on his back, worse than any black dog, and now he steered, his head began to toss from side to side and like a man exalted by drink he began to sing and chatter, whilst Rantan, who knew the Paumotuan mind and that in another minute the wheel would be dropped and the steersman loose and running amok, drew close.

Then suddenly, and with all the force of his body behind the blow, he struck and Sru fell like a pole-axed ox whilst the mate snapping at the spokes of the wheel steadied the vessel and stood, his eye on the binnacle cord holding the ship on her course.

Sru lay where he fell, just as Carlin lay where drink had struck him down; the fellows forward saw nothing, or if they did they made no movement, and the schooner, heeling deeper to the steadying breeze held on full south, whilst behind her the wake ran luminous with the gold of phosphorus and the silver of star-light.

Presently Sru sat up, then he rose to his feet. He remembered nothing, nothing of his terror or of the blow that had felled him; it seemed to him he must have fallen asleep at the wheel and that Rantan had relieved him.

XIII

South

The stars faded, the east grew crimson and the sun arose to show Levua gone; a sky without cloud, a sea without trace of sail or gull.

Le Moan, crouching in the bow with the risen sun hot on her left shoulder, saw the long levels of the marching swell as they came and passed, the *Kermadec* bowing to them; saw the distant southern sea line and beyond it the road to Karolin.

With her eyes shut and as the needle of the compass finds the north magnetic pole, she could have pointed to where Karolin lay; and as she gazed across the fields of the breeze-blown swell no trace of cloud troubled her mind, all was bright ahead. Sru had made it clear to her that no hurt would come to Taori, and with Peterson, had gone any last lingering doubt that may have been in her mind. She trusted Sru and she trusted Rantan, who had spoken kindly to her, Carlin, and the kanaka crew; of Peterson, the man who had terrified her first and the only trustable man on that ship, she had always had her doubts, begotten by that first impression, by his beard, his gruff voice and what Sru had said about Peterson and how he would "swallow all"—that is to say the pearls of Karolin; those mysterious pearls that the white men treasured and of which the charm hidden behind her ear had spoken to Sru.

She had always worn it as a protection and she had not the least doubt that it had spoken to Sru, just as a person might speak, and told him of those other pearls which she had often seen and played with when oysters were cast to rot on the beach for the sake of their shells. She had not the least doubt that to the talisman behind her ear was due this happy return and the elimination of Peterson. Was she wrong?

As she crouched, the back draught from the head sails fanning her hair, the ship and her crew, the sea and its waves, all vanished, dissolved matter from which grew as by some process of recrystallization the beach of Karolin. The long south beach where the sand was whispering in the wind, the hot south beach where the sun-stricken palms lifted their fronds to the brassy sky of noon and the tender skies of dawn and evening, the beach above which the stars stood at night all turning with the turning dome of sky.

She saw a canoe paddling ashore and the canoe man now on the beach, his eyes crinkled against the sun—eyes coloured like the sea when the grey of the squall mixes with its blue. The sun was on his red-gold hair and he trod the sands lightly, not as the kanaka walks and moves; one might have fancied little wings upon his feet.

His naked body against the blazing lagoon showed like a flame of gold against a flame of blue. It was Taori. Taori as she had seen him first, on that day when he had come to bid Aioma to the canoe building.

It was as if Fate on that day had suddenly stripped away a veil showing her the one thing to be desired, the only thing that would ever matter to her in this life or the next.

As she leaned, the breeze in her hair and her mind like a bird fleeting far ahead into the distance, flying fish like silver shaftless arrowheads passed and flittered into the blue water, and now a turtle floating asleep and disturbed by the warble of the bow wash and the creak of the onrushing schooner, sank quietly fathoms deep leaving only a few bubbles on the swell.

Carlin had come on deck. Rantan had said not a word about the broken open cupboard or the whiskey; the ship was cleared of drink and that was enough for him; when he came on deck a few minutes after the other, he found the beachcomber leaning on the after rail.

A shark was hanging in the wake of the schooner. A deep-sea ship does not sail alone. She gives company and shelter to all sorts of fish from the remora that hangs on for a whole voyage, to the bonito that follows her maybe for a week. In front of the shark, moving and glittering like spoon bait, a pilot fish showed in flashes of blue and gold.

Carlin turned from contemplation of these things to find Rantan at his side.

On going below for a wash after his night on deck, Carlin had found the other at breakfast. Neither man had spoken of the events of the night before, nor did they now.

"Following us steady, isn't he?" said Carlin, turning again to contemplate the monster in the wake—"don't seem to be swimming either and he's going all of eight knots. What's he after, following us like that?"

"Haven't you ever seen a shark before?" asked Rantan.

"Yes, and I've never seen good of them following a ship," replied Carlin, "and I'm not set on seeing them, 'specially now."

"Why now?" asked the mate.

But Carlin shied from the subject that was in both their minds.

"Oh, I don't know," said he, "I was thinking of the traverse in front of us. . . Say, now we're set and sailing for it, are you sure of hitting that island?"

"Sure," said the mate.

"Then you're better at the navigating job than you pretended to be," said Carlin. "What I like about you is the way you keep things hid."

"I've kept nothing hid," replied the other. "I'm crazy bad on the navigation, but I've got a navigator on board that'll take us there same as a bullet to a target."

"Sru?"

"Sru nothing—the kanaka girl, she's a Marayara. Ever heard of them? You get them among the kanakas; every kanaka has a pretty good sense of direction, but a Marayara, take him away from his island and he'll home back like a pigeon if he has a canoe and can paddle long enough. That island we took the girl from is the pearl island. Born and bred there she was, and it's her centre of everything. Sru got it all out of her and about the pearls and fixed up with her to take us back. Don't know what he's promised her, I reckon a few beads is all she wants and all she'll get, but that's how it lies: we've only got to push along due south by the compass and she'll correct us, leeway or set of current or any tomfool tricks of the needle don't matter to her. She never bothers about the compass, she sees where she wants to go straight before her nose, same's when land's in sight you see it and steer for it."

"Can she steer?" asked Carlin, who had not been on deck the day Sru set her at the wheel.

Rantan turned to where the girl was standing in the bow, called her aft and gave the wheel over to her. When she had felt the ship, standing with her head slightly uptilted, she altered the course a few points; the *Kermadec* had been off her path by that amount owing to leeway or set of current.

From that moment the ship was in the hands of Le Moan, tireless as only a being can be who exists always in the open air, she lived at the wheel with intervals for sleep and rest, always finding on her return the ship off her course, still heading south, but no longer on that exact and miraculous line drawn by instinct between herself and Karolin.

Error in the form of leeway or the influence of swell or the set of current could never push the vessel to east or west of that line, for the line moved with the ship, and as the journey shortened, like a steadily shortening string tied to a ball in centrifugal motion, it would bring the *Kermadec* at last to Karolin, no matter how far she was swung out of her course—blown fifty, a hundred, two hundred miles to east or west it would not matter, her head would turn to Karolin. The only flaw in that curious navigational instrument, the mind of Le Moan, was its blindness to distance from Karolin, the pull being the same for any distance, and had the island risen suddenly before them on some dark night, she would have piled the craft upon it unless warned by the sound of the reef.

RANTAN KEPT THE LOG GOING, he had a rough idea of the distance between Karolin and Levua, but he did not try to explain the log to Le Moan. If he had done so, his labour would have been wasted. Le Moan had no idea of time as we conceive it, cut up into hours, minutes and seconds. Time for her was a thing, not an abstract idea; a thing ever present yet shifting in appearance—energy.

The recognition of Time is simply the recognition of the rythm of energy by energy itself. Le Moan recognized the rhythm in the tides, in the sunrises and sunsets, in the going and coming of the fish shoals, in slumber and waking life, but of those figments of man's intellect, hours, minutes, years, she had no idea. Always in touch with reality, she had come in vague touch with the truth that there is no past, no future—nothing ever but rhythmic alternations of the present.

But, though unable to grasp the division of the real day into empirical fractions, the compass, that triumph of man's intellect, presented no difficulties to her. When Rantan explained its pointing to her she understood, the needle pointed away from Karolin.

The fleur-de-lys on the card, which seemed to her vaguely like the head of a fish spear, pointed away from Karolin, that is away from the south.

The compass card moved, she did not know that the compass card was absolutely steady, that this appearance of movement was a delusion caused by the altered course of the ship, that the ship pivoted on the card not the card on the ship.

If she let the ship off her course to the east, the card moved and her sense of direction told her at once that the fleur-de-lys was still pointing away from Karolin. She spoke on this matter to Sru. Sru, who had made the two voyages on ships and who was yet a capable steersman, had quite taken for granted his first captain's explanation to him of the compass; there was a god in it that held it just so and if Sru let the card wobble from the course set down, the god would most likely come out of the binnacle and kick Sru into the middle of next week. He was a Yankee skipper and he had made an excellent steersman of Sru.

Le Moan understood; she believed in gods, from Naniwa the shark-toothed one to Nan the benign: believed in them, just as white men believe in their Gods—with reservations; but this was different from anything she had hitherto conceived of a deity. He must be very small to be contained in the binnacle, very small and set of purpose always pointing with the spear head away from Karolin. Why?

Rantan had pointed down to the spear head and away north and told her it always pointed there, always away from the direction of Karolin. Why?

She had not asked him why the card moved, or seemed to move, Sru having already told her.

The feeling came to her that the little imprisoned something was against going to Karolin, but no one seemed to mind it, yet they were always consulting it, Rantan when he took the wheel and Sru and Maru, who was also a good steersman.

Everyday at noon Rantan would appear on deck and take an observation of the sun with Peterson's sextant, whilst Carlin, if he were on deck, would cuff himself on the thigh and turn and lean over the rail to laugh unobserved.

Rantan was only fooling—keeping up appearances, so that the crew might fancy him as good as Peterson in finding his way on the sea. Sru had never told the others that they depended entirely on Le Moan, the fact that she was a way-finder was known to them, but it is as well for the after guard to keep up appearances. Rantan might as well have been looking at the sun through a beer bottle for all he knew of the matter, but the crew could not tell that. So, as a navigator, he held a place in their minds above the girl.

At night when the binnacle lamp was lit and she happened to be at the wheel, her eyes would wander to the trembling card. She would put the ship a bit off its course just to see it move, noticing that it always moved in the same manner in a reverse direction to the alteration in course. If the head of the schooner turned to starboard, the card would rotate to port and vice versa. She studied its doings as one studies the doings of a strange animal, but she never caught it altering its mind or its action.

At night it always seemed to her that the thing in the binnacle, whether god or devil, was inimical to her, or at all events warning her not to take the ship back to Karolin; by day it did not matter.

So under the stars and over the phosphorescent sea the *Kermadec* headed south, ever south, the blazing dawns leaping over the port rail and the gigantic sunsets dying with the blood of Titans the skies to starboard, till one morning Le Moan, handing the wheel to Rantan, pointed ahead and then walked forward. Her work was done. Far ahead, paling the sky, shone the lagoon blaze of Karolin.

BOOK II

I

THE MAID OF AIOMA

Le Moan had left Karolin as a gull leaves the reef, unnoticed.

Not a soul had seen her go and it was not for some days that Aioma, busy with the tree felling, recollected her existence, and the fact that she had not followed him to the northern beach; then he sent a woman across and she had returned with news that there was no trace of the girl though her canoe was beached, also that there was no trace of food having been recently cooked, and that the girl must have been gone some days as there were no recent sand traces. The wind even when it is only moderately strong blurs and obliterates sand traces, and the woman judged that no one had been about on the southern beach for some days. She had found tracks, however, for which she could not account. The marks left by the boots of Peterson, also the footsteps of the kanakas who had carried the water casks disturbed her mind; they had nearly vanished, but it seemed to her that many people had been there, a statement that left Aioma cold.

Aioma had no time for fancies. If the girl were alive, she would come across in her canoe, if death had come to her in any of the forms in which death walked the reef, there was no use in troubling. The call to the canoe building, resented at first, had given him new youth, the spirit of the sea sang in him and the perfume of the new-felled trees brought Uta Matu walking on the beach, and his warriors.

Aioma, like Le Moan, had no use for the past or the future, the burning present was everything.

Things that had been were to Aioma things floating alongside at a greater or less distance, not astern. It was not the memory of Uta Matu that walked the beach, but Uta Matu himself, untouchable, because of distance, and only able to talk as he had talked in life, but still there. Aioma had not to turn his head to look backwards at him as we have to turn our heads to see our dead, he had only to glance sideways, as it were. The things of yesterday, the day before yesterday and the day before that, were beside Aioma at greater or less distances, not behind him—all like surf riders on the same wave with him and carried forward by the same flowing, yet ever separating one from the other though keeping in line.

In the language of Karolin there was no word indicating our idea of the past except the word *akuma* (distance) which might mean the distance between a canoe and a canoe or between a happening of today and of yesterday, and to the woman who judged that Le Moan had not trod the beach for some days, "days" meant measures of distance, not of time. Le Moan had been travelling, moving away from the beach, not returning, whilst so many sunrises had occurred and so many sunsets. She had been away a long distance, not a long time.

The speed of a man running a mile on Karolin had nothing to do with the time occupied, it was a measure of his strength; the race was a struggle between the man and the mile, and of the runners the swiftest to a Karalonite was not the quickest but the strongest and most agile; this profound truth was revealed to their instinctive sight undimmed by the *muscæ volitantes* which we call minutes, seconds and hours, also the truth that when the race was over it was not extinct but merely removed to a distance—just as a canoe drifting from a canoe is not extinct though untouchable and out of hail, and fading at last from sight through distance.

A dead man on Karolin was a man who had drifted away; he was there, but at a distance, he might even return through the distance in a stronger way than memory sight could reveal him! Many had. Uta Matu himself had been seen in this way by several since he had drifted away—he had come back once to tell Nalia the wife of Oti where the sacred paddle was hid, the paddle which acted as the steer oar of the biggest war canoe. He had forgotten that the war canoe had been destroyed. Still he had returned. Though with a Melanesian strain in them, unlike the Melanesians the men of Karolin had no belief that the souls of ancestors become reincarnated in fish or birds, nor did they believe in the influence of *Mana,* that mysterious spiritual something believed in so widely by Polynesians and Melanesians alike.

Memory, to the Karolinite, was a sort of sight which enabled the living to look not over the past but the present, and see the people and things that floated, not behind in a far-off past, but to right and left in a far-off present.

Just as the surf rider sees his companions near and far, all borne on the same wave, though some might be beyond reach of voice, and some almost invisible through distance, the return of a spirit was an actual moving of a distant one towards the seer, as though a surf rider were to strike out and swim to a far-off fellow at right angles to the flow of the wave.

So Aioma, as he worked, saw Uta Matu and his warriors and the old canoe-builders, not as dead and gone figures, but as realities though beyond touch and hail of voice and sight of the eye of flesh.

SINCE THE WAR, YEARS AGO, between the northern and southern tribes, a large proportion of the children born on the island had been boys, whilst most of the women had developed manly attributes in accordance with that natural law which rules in the remotest island as well as in the highest and broadest civilization.

Aioma had no need of helpers, leaving out the boys, some dozen or so, who could wield an ax as well as a man; but Aioma though his heart and soul were in his work was no mere canoe-builder. He had in him the making of a statesman. He would not let Dick work at the building or do any work at all except fishing and fish spearing.

"You are the chief (Ompalu)," said Aioma as he sat of an evening before the house of Uta Matu, now the house of Dick. "You are young and do not know all the ways of things, but I love you as a son; I do not know what is in you that is above us, but the sea I love is in your eyes. The sea, our father, sent you, but you have still to learn the ways of the land, where the chief does no work." Then he would grunt to himself and rock as he sat, and then his voice rising to a whine, "Could the people raise their heads to one who labours with them, or would they bow their heads so that he might put his foot on their necks?" Then casting his eyes down he would talk to himself, the words so run together as to be indistinguishable; but always, Katafa noticed, his eyes would return again and again to the little ships in the shadow of the house, the model ships made by Kearney long ago—the vestiges of a civilization of which Dick and Aioma and Katafa knew nothing, or only that the ships, the big ships of which these were the likenesses, were dangerous and the men in them evil and to be avoided or destroyed if possible.

The *Portsey* of long ago that had fired a cannon shot and destroyed Katafa's canoe, the schooner that had brought the Melanesians to Palm Tree, the Spanish ship that had been sunk in Karolin lagoon and the whaler that had come after her, all these had burnt into the minds of Dick, Aioma and Katafa; the fact that something of which they did not know the name (but which was civilization), was out there beyond the sea line, something that, octopus-like, would at times thrust out a feeler in the form of a ship, an *ayat* destructive and, if possible, to be destroyed.

Ayat was the name given by Karolin to the great burgomaster gulls that were to the small gulls what schooners are to canoes, and so anything in the form of a ship was an *ayat*, that is to say, a thing carrying with it all the propensities of a robber and a murderer; for the great gulls would rob the lesser gulls of their food and devour their chicks and fight and darken the sunshine of the reef with their wings.

The comparison was not a compliment to the Pacific traders or their ships or the civilization that had sent them forth to prey on the world, but it was horribly apposite.

And yet the little *ayats* in the shadow of the house had for Aioma an attraction beyond words. They were as fascinating as sin. This old child after a hard day's work would sometimes dream of them in his sleep; dream that he was helping to sail them on the big rock pool, as he sometimes did in reality. The frigate, the full-rigged ship, the schooner and the whale man, all had cruised in the rock pool which seemed constructed by nature as a model testing tank; indeed the first great public act of Dick as ruler of the Karolinites had been a full review of this navy on the day after he had fetched Aioma from the southern beach. Aioma, fascinated by the sight of the schooner which Dick had shown him on his landing, had insisted on seeing the others launched and the whole population had stood round ten deep with the little children between the women's legs, all with their eyes fixed on the pretty sight. The strangest sight—for Kearney the illiterate and ignorant had managed to symbolize the two foundations of civilization, war and trade; and here in little yet in essence lay the ships of Nelson and the ships of Villeneuve: the great wool ships, the *Northumberland* that had brought Dick's parents to Palm Tree, the whalers of Marthas Vineyard and the sandalwood schooners, those first carriers of the disease of the white man.

To Aioma the schooner was the most fascinating. He knew the whaler with her try works and her heavy davits and her squat build; he had seen her before in the whaler whose brutal crew had landed and been driven off. He knew the ship, he had seen its likeness in the Spanish ship of long ago; the frigate intrigued him, but the schooner took his heart—it was not only that he understood her rig and way of sailing better than the rig and way of sailing of the others, it was more than that. Aioma was an instinctive ship lover, and to the lover of ships, the schooner has most appeal, for the schooner is of all things that float the most graceful and the most beautiful; and in contrast to her canvas, the canvas of your square rigged ship becomes dishcloths hung out to dry.

He brooded on this thing over which Kearney had expended his most loving care, and in which nothing was wanting. He understood the topping lifts that supported the main boom, the foresail, the use of the standing rigging. Kearney, through his work, was talking to him and just as Kearney had explained this and that to Dick, so Dick was explaining it to Aioma. Truly a man can speak though dead, even as Kearney was speaking now.

The method of reefing a sail was unknown to Aioma; a canoe sail was never reefed, reduction of canvas was made by tying the head of the sail up to spill the wind. Fore canvas was unknown to Aioma, but he understood.

The subconscious mathematician in him that made him able to build great canoes capable of standing heavy weather and carrying forty or fifty men apiece, understood all about the practice of the business, though he had never heard of centres of rotation, absolute or relative velocities, of impelling powers, or the laws of the collision of bodies; of inertia or pressures of resistance or squares of velocity or series of inclinations.

Squatting on his hams before the little model of the *Rarotanga*, he knew nothing of these things and yet he knew that the schooner was good, that she would sail close to the wind with little leeway when the wind was on the beam, that the rudder was better than the steering paddle, that the sail area though great would not capsize her, that she was miles ahead of anything he had ever made in the form of a ship. That the maker of the *ayat* was a genius beside whom he was a duffer, unknowing that Kearney was absolutely without inventive genius, and that the schooner was the work of a million men extending over three thousand years.

Katafa sitting beside Dick would watch Aioma as he brooded and played with the thing. It had no fascination for her. The little ships had always repelled her if anything. They were the only dividing point between her and Dick—she could not feel his pleasure or interest in them, and from this fact possibly arose a vague foreboding that perhaps some day in some way the little ships might seperate them. When a woman loves, she can become jealous of a man's pipe, of his tennis racket, of his best friend, of anything that she can't share and which occupies his attention at times more than she does.

But the essence of jealousy is concentration, and Katafa's green eye was cast not so much on the whole fleet as on the little schooner. This was Dick's favourite, as it was Aioma's.

ONE NIGHT, LONG AFTER THE vanishing of Le Moan, so long that everyone had nearly forgotten her, Aioma had a delightful dream.

He dreamt that he was only an inch high and standing on the schooner's deck. Dick reduced to the same stature was with him, and half a dozen others, and the schooner was in the rock pool that had spread to the size of Karolin lagoon. Oh, the joy of that business! They were hauling up the mainsail and up it went to the pull of the halyards just as he had often hauled it with the pull of his finger and thumb on the tiny halyards of the model; but this was a real great sail and men had to pull hard to raise it and there it was set. Then the foresail went up and the jib was cast loose and Aioma, mad with joy, was at the tiller, the tiller that he had often moved with his finger and thumb.

Then pressed by the wind she began to heel over and the outrigger—she had taken on an outrigger—went into the air; he could see the outrigger gratings with drinking-nuts and bundles of food tied to it after the fashion of sea-going canoes, and he shouted to his companions to climb on to it and bring it down. Then he awoke, sweating but dazzled by the first part of the dream.

Two days later a boy came running and shouting to him as he was at work; and turning, Aioma saw the fulfilment of his vision. Borne by the flooding tide with all sails drawing and a bone in her teeth, the little schooner swelled to a thousand times her size, was gaily entering the lagoon. It was the *Kermadec*.

II

WAR

Rantan was at the wheel, and Le Moan forward, with swelling heart, stood watching as they passed the break, the Gates of Morning, through which the tide was flooding like a mill-race. She saw the southern beach still deserted and the northern beach where the trees sheltered the village from sight. Not a sign of life was to be seen in all that vast prospect of locked lagoon and far-running reefs till from the distant trees a form appeared—Aioma.

After him came others till the beach close to the trees was thronged by a crowd even in movement like a colony of ants disturbed and showing now against the background of the trees the glint of spears. Le Moan's heart sank under a sudden premonition of evil. She turned and glanced to where Rantan at the wheel was staring ahead and Carlin close by him was shading his eyes.

Rantan had not expected this. He had fancied Karolin deserted. Sru had said nothing of what Le Moan had told him about Taori and he said nothing now as he stood with eyes wrinkled against the sun blaze from the lagoon. Taori, he had gathered to be some kanaka boy, a love of Le Moan's who, so far from giving trouble, would welcome her back— but that crowd, its movements and the flash of the thready spears! He made vague answers to the questions flung at him by the mate, then at the order to let go the anchor he ran forward whilst Carlin dived below, returning with two of the Veterli rifles and ammunition. Then as the anchor fell and the *Kermadec* swung to her moorings on the flood, nose to the break, Rantan, leaving the wheel and standing with compressed lips, his hand on the after rail and his eyes on the crowd, suddenly broke silence and turned to Carlin.

"We don't want any fighting," said he. "We've got to palaver them. It's a jolt. Peterson said the place was empty, and I reckon he lied or else he didn't keep his eyes skinned, but whether or no we've got to swallow it. Worst is we've no trade to speak of, nothing but sandalwood. No matter   we don't want nothing but to be left alone. Order out the boat and we'll row off to them, and keep those guns hid."

He went below for Peterson's revolver which Carlin had forgotten, and when he returned, the boat was down with four kanakas for crew and Carlin in the stern sheets; he followed and took his place by the beachcomber and the boat pushed off.

He had made a great blunder, absolutely forgotten the existence of Le Moan and her use as an ambassador, but the mind of Rantan was working against odds.

He had never consciously worried about Peterson. The dead Peterson was done with out of count, and yet away in the back of his mind Peterson existed, not as a form, not even as a shadow, but as the vaguest, vaguest hint of possible trouble, some day. Steering, or smoking below, or enjoying in prospect the profits to be got out of the venture, Rantan would be conscious of a something that was marring his view of things; something that, seizing it with his mind, would prove to be nothing more than just a feeling that trouble might come some day owing to Peterson.

On sailing into the lagoon, the wind across that great blue pearl garden had swept his mind clear of all trace of worry. Here was success at last, wealth for the taking and no one to watch the taker or interfere with his doings. No one but the gulls. A child on that beach would have shattered the desolation and destroyed the feeling of security and detachment from the world.

Then the trees had given up their people and to Rantan it was almost as though Peterson himself had reappeared.

He had reckoned to get rid of the crew of the *Kermadec* in his own given time after he had worked them for his profit, to get rid of Carlin, of his own name, of everything and anything that could associate him with this venture, and here were hundreds of witnesses where he had expected to find none but the gull that cannot talk.

Truly it was a jolt!

As the boat drew on for the shore, the crowd on the beach moved and spread and contracted and then became still, the spears all in one clump.

There were at least thirty of the boys of Karolin able to hurl a spear with the precision of a man, and when Aioma had sighted the schooner and given the alarm, Dick, who had been on the outer beach, had called them together. Taiepa, the son of Aioma, had distributed the spears and Aioma himself in a few rapid words had fired the hearts of the tribe.

The strangers must not be allowed to land. For a moment, but only a moment, he took the command of things from Dick's hands. "They came before," said Aioma, "when I was a young man, and the great Uta knowing them to be men full of evil would not allow them to land but drove them off, and yet again they came in a canoe bigger than the first (the Spanish ship), and they landed and fought with Uta and he killed them and burnt their great canoe—and yet again they have come and yet again we must fight. We are few, but Taori in himself is many."

"They shall not land," said Dick, "even if I face them alone."

That was the temper of Karolin and it voiced itself as the boat drew closer to the beach in a cry that rang across the water, harsh and sudden, making the kanaka rowers pause and turn their heads.

"They mean fighting," said Carlin, bending towards one of the rifles lying on the bottom boards.

"Leave that gun alone," said Rantan.

He ordered the rowers to pull a bit closer, rising up and standing in the stern sheets and waving his hand to the beach crowd as though intimating that he wished to speak to them.

The only answer was a spear flung by Taiepa that came like a flash of light and fell into the water true of aim but short by a few yards. The rowers stopped again and backed water. Whilst Carlin picked up the floating spear as a trophy and put it with the rifles, Rantan sat down. Then he ordered them to pull ahead altering the helm so that the bow turned away from the shore and to the west.

As they moved along the beach the distant crowd followed, but the mate did not heed it; he was busy taking notes of the lie of the land, and the position of the trees. The trees, though deep enough to hide the village from the break, were nowhere dense enough to give efficient cover; the reef just here was very broad but very low. A man would be a target—the head and shoulders of him at least—even if he were on the outer coral.

Rantan having obtained all the information he required on these matters altered the course of the boat and made back for the ship.

"Aren't you going to have one single shot at them?" asked the disgusted Carlin.

"You wait a while," replied the other.

When they reached the *Kermadec* he ordered the men to remain in the boat, and going on board dropped down below with his companion. He went to the locker where the ammunition was stored and counted the boxes. There were two thousand rounds.

"I reckon that will do," said Rantan. "You said you were a good shot. Well, you've got a chance to prove your words. I'm going to shoot up this lagoon."

"From the ship?"

"Ship, no, the boat's good enough; they have no cover worth anything and only a few old fishing canoes that aren't good enough to attack us in."

"Well, I'm not saying you're wrong," said Carlin, "but seems to me it will be more than a one-day job."

"We aren't hustled for time," replied the other, "not if it took weeks."

They came on deck, each carrying a box of ammunition, the spear salved by Carlin had been brought on board by him and stood against the rail. Neither man noticed it, nor did they notice Le Moan crouched in the doorway of the galley and seeming to take shelter from the sun.

Carlin who had ordered a water breaker to be filled, lowered it himself into the boat, then getting in followed by the mate the boat pushed off, Sru rowing stern oar and Rantan at the yoke lines.

It was close on midday and the great sun directly overhead poured his light on the lagoon; beyond the crowd and the trees on the northern beach the coral ran like a white road for miles and miles, to be lost in a smoky shimmer, and from the reef came the near and far voice of the breakers on the outer beach.

The crew left on board, some six in number, had dropped into the foc'sle to smoke and talk. Le Moan could hear their voices as she rose and stood at the rail, her eyes fixed on the boat and her mind divided between the desire to cast herself into the water and swim to the reef and the instinct which told her to stay and watch and wait.

She knew what a rifle was. She had seen Peterson practising with one of the Viterlis at a floating bottle. There were rifles in the boat, but it was not the rifles that filled her mind with a foreboding amounting to terror, it was Rantan's face as he returned and as he left again. And she could do nothing.

Carlin, before lowering the water breaker had handed an ax into the boat. Why? She could not tell, nor why the water breaker had been taken. It was all part of something that she could not understand, something that was yet evil and threatening to Taori.

She could not make his figure out amongst the crowd, it was too far, and yet he was surely there.

She watched.

HENRY DE VERE STACPOOLE

The boat drew on towards the beach. Then at the distance of a couple of hundred yards the oarsmen ceased rowing and she floated idly and scarcely drifting—for it was slack water, the flood having ceased. One might have thought the men on board of her were fishing or just lazing in the sun—anything but the truth.

Then Le Moan saw a tiny puff of smoke from the boat's side, a figure amongst the crowd on the beach sprang into the air and fell, and on the still air came the far-off crack of a rifle.

Carlin had got his man. He was an indifferent shot but he could scarcely have missed as he fired into the brown of the crowd. Rantan, no better a shot, fired immediately after and by some miracle nobody was hit.

Then as Le Moan watched, she saw the crowd break to pieces and vanish amongst the trees, leaving only two figures on the beach, one lying on the sands and one standing erect and seeming to threaten the boat with upflung arm. It was Taori. Her sight as though it had gained telescopic power told her at once that it was Taori.

She saw him bend and catch up the fallen figure in his arms and as he turned to the trees with it, the boat fired again, but missed him. Another shot rang out before he reached the trees, but he vanished unscathed, and quiet fell on the beach and lagoon, broken only by the clamour of gulls disturbed by the firing.

Le Moan changed her place, the ebb was beginning to run and the schooner to swing with it. She came forward and took her position near the foc'sle head, her eyes still fixed on the boat and beach. From the foc'sle came the sound of an occasional snore from the kanakas who had turned in and were sleeping like dogs.

Four fishing canoes lay on the sands near the trees, and now as she watched, she saw the boat under way again pulling in to the beach. The rowers tumbled out and the boat pushed off a few yards with only the two white men in her whilst the landing party made for the canoes and began to smash them up.

Sru—she could tell him by his size—wielded the ax, two others helped in the business with great lumps of loose coral, whilst the fourth stood watch.

It took time, for they did their work thoroughly, breaking the outriggers, breaking the outrigger poles, breaking the canoe bodies, working with the delight that children take in sheer destruction.

The god Destruction was abroad on Karolin beach and lagoon. Though without a temple or a place in mythology of all the gods, he is the most powerful, the most agile and quick of eye, and the swiftest to come when called.

Le Moan watching, saw the four men on the beach stand contemplating their work before returning to the boat.

Then she saw one of them throw up his hands and fall as if felled by an ax. The others turned to run and the foremost of them tripped as a man trips on a kink in a carpet and fell; of the two others one pitched and turned a complete somersault as though some unseen jiu-jitsu player had dealt with him, and the fourth crumpled like a suddenly closed concertina.

Le Moan's heart sprang alive in her. She knew. The terrible arrows of Karolin poisoned with argora that kills with the swiftness and more than certainty of a bullet had, fired from the trees, done their work.

The spear was the favourite weapon of Karolin, not the bow. The bow was used only on occasions and at long distances. When they came down to resist the landing of Rantan, they had come armed with spears; driven to the shelter of the trees, Aioma, the artful one, had remembered the bows stowed in one of the canoe houses. It was years since the arrows had been poisoned, but the poison of argora never dies, nor does it weaken with time.

In four swings of a pendlum the arrows had done their work, and four upstanding men lay stretched on the beach, motionless, for this terrible poison striking at the nerve centres kills in two beats of the pulse.

Rantan and Carlin, close enough to see the flight of the arrows, put wildly out, tugging at the heavy oars and rowing for their lives; a few hundred yards off shore they paused, rested on their oars and took counsel.

It was a bad business.

Armed with rifles and with easy range they had only managed to bag one of the enemy, whereas. . . !

"Hell," said Carlin.

The sweat was running down his broad face. Rantan, brooding, said nothing for a moment. Then suddenly he broke silence.

"We've dished their canoes, they can't come out and attack us; we've got the range over them, those arrows are no use at any distance; they live mostly on fish, those chaps, and they can't come out and fish, having no canoes, and we aren't hurried for time." He seemed talking to himself, adding up accounts, whilst Carlin, who had picked up one of the rifles, sat with it across his knees, his face turned shoreward where on the beach lay the four dead men, and save for the gulls not a sign of life. The boat on the ebb tide was drifting slowly back in the direction of the schooner.

"We've just got to row up along," went on Rantan, "and get level with the trees. Those trees don't give much shelter across the reef. Their houses wouldn't stop a bullet from a popgun. Take your oar, when we've got our position we can anchor and take things quiet."

Carlin, putting his gun down, took his oar and they began pulling the heavy boat against the current till they got opposite the village and the trees.

Then within rifle shot, but beyond the reach of arrow flight, they dropped the anchor and the boat swung to the current and broadside to the shore.

Rantan was right—the trees though dense enough in patches were not a sufficient cover for a crowd of people, and the houses were death traps. From where they lay they could see the little houses clear marked against the sky beyond and the house of Uta Matu with the post beside it on top of which was the head of Nan, god of the coconut trees, Nan the benign watching over his people, the puraka beds and the pandanus palms.

Of old there had been two gods of Karolin, Nan the benign and Naniwa the ferocious.

Le Moan's mother had been Le Jennabon, daughter of Le Juan, priestess of Naniwa the shark-toothed god. On the death of Le Juan, Naniwa had seemed to depart, for Karolin. Had he? Do the gods ever die whilst there is a human heart to give them sanctuary?

Nan the benign, grinning on his post—he was carved from a coconut—was set in such a way that his face was turned to the east, that is to say towards the gates of morning. He was placed in that way according to ritual. Chance had anchored the schooner in his line of vision. Hand helpless, as are most benign things, poor old Nan could do nothing to protect the people he no doubt loved. He could keep the weazle-teazle worms away from the puraka plants and he could help a bit in bringing up rain, and it was considered that he could even protect the canoes from the cobra worms that devour planking; but against the wickedness of man and Viterli rifles he was useless.

And yet today as he gazed across at the schooner, his grin was in no way diminished, and as the wind stirred the cane post he waggled his head jauntily, perhaps because on the deck of the schooner he saw the granddaughter of the priestess of the shark-toothed god and said to himself with a thrill and a shudder: "Naniwa has returned."

In the old days when a man revenged himself for some wrong, or, going mad, dashed out the brains of another with a club, he was supposed to be possessed by Naniwa, for just as Nan was the minister of agriculture, the shark-toothed one was the minister of justice. He was in a way the law executing criminals and also making criminals for execution, just as the law does with us.

Anyhow and at all events and bad as he may have been, he was the sworn enemy of foreigners; he had inspired Uta Matu to attack the whaler and he had inspired Le Juan in calling for the attack on the Spanish ship of long ago and today perhaps he had inspired Aioma in resisting the landing of these newcomers. The battle was still in the balance, but there on the deck of the anchored schooner stood the granddaughter of his priestess darkly brooding, helpless for the moment, but watching and waiting to strike.

No wonder that Nan grinned and waggled his head at her with a click-clocking noise, for the coconut had worked a bit loose on its stick.

RANTAN TOOK HIS SEAT ON the bottom boards in the stern, resting his rifle comfortably on the gunnel; Carlin, going forward, did the same. The wind which had risen and which was moving Nan on his post, stirred the foliage, and between the boles and over the bushes of mammee apple the shifting shadows danced and the shafts of light showered, but sign of human being there was none.

The crafty Aioma, through the mouth of Dick, had ordered all the children and young people into the mammee apple and the women into the houses whilst he and Dick had taken shelter behind trees, two vast trees that stood like giants amidst the coconuts and pandanas palms, brothers of the trees growing further along the reef that were being used for canoe building.

Aioma knew from old experience what white men could do with guns, but he did not know that a house wall capable of stopping an arrow was incapable of stopping a rifle bullet.

Rantan seeing nothing else to fire at aimed at one of the houses, fired, and as the smoke cleared saw, literally, the house burst open.

The women poured out through the broken canes, made as if to run along the reef to the west and were suddenly headed back by a figure armed with a canoe paddle. It was Dick. He drove them into the mammee apple, where they took cover with the others, then running to the second house of refuge, whilst the bullets whizzed around him, he bade the women in it lie down, calling to the other hidden women to do the same, and then taking shelter himself.

But the blunder of Aioma was fatal. The men in the boat knew now for certain that the mammee apple thickets were packed, that there were no pot holes or crevasses of any account on the seaward side of the reef, that they had the population of Karolin corralled.

Resting his rifle carefully on the gunnel, Rantan led off. He couldn't well miss, and the deafening explosion of the rifle was followed by a shriek and a movement in the distant bushes where some unfortunate had been hit, and, striving to rise, had been pulled down by his or her companions.

Carlin laughed and fired and evidently missed, to judge by the silence that followed the shot.

Rantan had some trouble with a cartridge. His face had quite changed within the last few minutes and since the corralling of the natives was assured. It was like a mask and the upper lip projected as though suddenly swollen by some injury. He flung the defective cartridge away, loaded with another and fired.

The shot was followed by the cry of a woman and the wailing of a child. One could guess that the child had been hit, not the woman it belonged to, for the wailing kept on and on, a sound shocking in that solitude where nothing was to be seen but the empty beach, the line of mammee apple and the glimpse of empty sea beyond and through the trees.

Carlin, more brutal but less terrible than Rantan, laughed. He was about to fire when a form suddenly moving and breaking from the trees took his eye and stayed his hand.

It was Dick. In his left hand he held a bow and in his right a sheaf of arrows. Aioma had directed that before taking cover the bows and arrows should be laid by the westermost of the two big trees that he and Dick had chosen for shelter. Dick had only to stretch out his arm to seize the weapons and armed with them he came, leaving shelter behind him, right into the open and on to the sands.

At the cry of the first victim, he had started and shivered all over like a dog; at the voice of the child thought left him, or only the thought that there, amongst the bushes with the children and the women, was

Katafa; seizing a bow and a handful of the arrows, he left the tree and came out on to the beach and right down to the waterside.

There were seven arrows. He cast them on the sand, picked up one and fixed it with the notch in the bow-string; as he did so Carlin, altering his aim from the bushes to this new target, fired. The sand spurted a yard to the right of the bowman, who, drawing the arrow till the barb nearly touched the bow shaft, loosed it.

It fell true in line but yards short, and as it flicked the water, Rantan's bullet came plung into the sand and only three inches from Dick's right foot.

Dick laughed. Like Rantan's, his face was transfigured.

He had come with no instinct but to draw the fire away from the bushes to himself. Now, in a moment, he had forgotten everything but the boat and the men in the boat and the burning hatred that, could it have been loosed, would have destroyed them like a thunderbolt.

Bending and picking up another arrow he loosed it, increasing the elevation. This time it did not fall short, it went over the boat, zipping down and into the water from the blue several yards away in the lagoon side.

"Hell," said Carlin.

He dropped the rifle in his hands and seized on the anchor rope, dragging up the anchor, whilst Rantan, firing hurriedly and without effect, seized an oar.

Poisoned arrows even when shot wildly and at random are not things to be played with, and as they rowed, the fear of death in their hearts, came another arrow—wide but only a yard to starboard; then came another short and astern.

"We're out of range," said Carlin. They let the boat drift a moment. Another arrow came, but well astern.

Then with a yell as if the silent devil in the soul of him had spoken at last, Rantan sprang to his feet and shook his fist at the figure on the beach.

Then they dropped the anchor and took up the rifles. The boat was out of arrow range, but the bushes were still a clear target for the rifles.

Like artists who know their limitations, the two gunmen turned their attention from the single figure on the beach to the greater target, and Dick, who on seeing the boat draw off beyond range, stood without shooting anymore, victorious for the moment but waiting.

He saw the anchor cast over, he saw the boatmen taking up their positions again, he saw the thready tubes of the guns and knew that the firing was about to recommence, then, bending, he seized an arrow and clasping it with the bow in his left hand, rushed into the water. Swimming with his right arm, he headed straight for the boat.

Dick in the water was a fish. To get close to the boat, and, treading water or even floating, loose the arrow at short range, was his object. He was no longer a man nor a human being, but implacable enmity, reasonless energy directed by hate.

Rantan and Carlin had fired before they saw what was coming, a head, an arm half submerged and a bow skittering along the water. Carlin's jaws snapped together, he tried to extract the cartridge case from his gun, fumbled and failed.

Rantan, less rattled and quicker with his fingers, extracted and reloaded, aimed and fired and missed.

"Fire, you damned fool": he said to the other, but the game was lost—Carlin was at the anchor rope, the memory of the four dead men on the beach slain by the poisoned arrows of Karolin had him in its grip as it had the other, who with one last glance at the coming terror dropped his gun and seized an oar.

They were beaten, put to flight—if only for the moment.

III

The Return to the *Kermadec*

As they rowed making for the schooner with the light of the westering sun in their eyes, they could see the head of the swimmer as he made back for the shore, and away on the beach near the trees they could see the great gulls congregated around the forms of the four dead men, a boiling of wings above the reef line and against the evening blue of the sky.

Predatory gulls when feeding on a carcase do not sit and gorge, they are always in motion more or less, especially when they are in great numbers as now. Far at sea and maybe from a hundred miles away guests were still arriving for the banquet spread by death—late comers whose voices went before them sharp on the evening wind, or came up against it weak, remote and filled with suggestions of hunger and melancholy.

"God's truth," said the beachcomber, spitting as he rowed.

They were coming on towards the ship and it was the first word spoken.

They had defeat behind them, and even if it were only momentary defeat, ahead of them lay explanations. How would the remainder of the crew take the killing of Sru and his companions? There was also the fact that they had lost four divers.

The *Kermadec* was close to them now but not a soul showed on her deck, not even Le Moan, who on sighting the returning boat had slipped into the galley where she sat crouched in a corner by the copper with eyes closed as if asleep.

She had told the fellows below that she would warn them on the return of the boat. She had forgotten her promise, her mind was far away, travelling, circling in a nebulous world like a bird lost in a fog, questing for a point to rest on. She knew well that though the boat was returning, this was not the end of things. Tomorrow it would all begin again, the destroyed canoes, the implacable firing from the boat; the face of Rantan as he pushed off all told her this. Crouching, with closed eyes, she heard the oars, the slight grinding of the boat as it came alongside and the thud of bare feet as Carlin came over the side on to the deck. No voices.

The beachcomber had taken in the situation at a glance, the crew were down below, smoking or sleeping, leaving the schooner to look after herself. It was just as well—down there they would have heard nothing of the distant firing, seen nothing of the killing. He knew kanakas, knew as well as though he had been told that as soon as he and Rantan had pushed off, the crew had taken charge of the foc'sle.

Leaving Rantan to tie up, he went below to the cabin for some food, where, a moment later, the mate joined him.

In a few minutes, their hunger satisfied, they began to speak and almost at once they were wrangling.

"Shooting up the lagoon—well, you've shot it up and much good it has done us," said Carlin. "I'm not against killing, but seems to me the killing has been most on their side. What's the use of talking? It will take a year at this game to do any good and how are you to manage it from the boat?"

"Tomorrow," said Rantan, "I'll move the ship up, anchor her off that village and then we'll see. Chaps won't come swimming out to attack a ship, and we can pot them from the deck till they put their hands up. We've no time to wipe them all off, but I reckon a few days of the business will break them up and once a kanaka is broken, he's broken."

Carlin without replying got into his bunk and stretching at full length, lit his pipe; as he flung the Swedish match box to Rantan, a sound from the deck above like the snap of a broken stick, made him raise his eyes towards the skylight. Rantan, the box in his hand paused for a moment, then the sound not being repeated, he lit his pipe.

Throwing the box back to the other he came on deck.

The deck was still empty, but the spear that had been leaning against the rail was gone. Rantan did not notice this, he came forward passing the galley without looking in and stopped at the foc'sle hatch to listen.

One of the strange things about sea-going kanakas is their instinct to get together in any old hole or corner out of sight of the deck, the sea, the land and the sky, and in an atmosphere that would choke a European, frowst.

The fellows below were just waking up after a catnap and the fume of Blue Bird, the old tobacco of the old Pacific days sold at two cents a stick, was rising from the hatch mixed with the sound of voices engaged in talk; they had heard nothing of the firing, if they had they would not have bothered; they had no idea of the fate of Sru and his companions, if they had they would not have much cared. Time was, for these men, the moment; unspeculative as birds they took life with a terrible light-heartedness scarcely human in its acceptance of all things: blows or bananas, the righteousness or the rascality of the white man.

Rantan rapped on the hatch and called on them to tumble up. Then when he had them all on deck, the sunset on their faces and fear of what he might say to them for leaving the schooner to take charge of herself in their hearts, he began to talk to them as only he knew how.

Not a word of abuse. The natives of this island were bad men who had treacherously killed Sru and his companions who had landed to talk with them. In return, he, Rantan, had killed many of them and destroyed their canoes. Tomorrow he intended to bring the ship further up towards the village, and with the speak-sticks kill more of them. Meanwhile the crew could go below and enjoy themselves as they liked, leaving one on deck to keep watch on the weather. There was no danger from the beach as all the canoes had been destroyed. Then he dismissed them and went aft.

IV

The Mind of Kanoa and the Rising Moon

The crew, numbering now only six, and deprived of the leadership of Sru, watched Rantan go aft and disappear down the saloon hatch, then they fell to discussing the fate of Sru and his companions. The lost men were from Soma, of the remainder two were from Nanuti in the Gilberts, the rest were Paumotuans hailing from Vana Vana and Haraikai. The loss of the others did not affect them much, nor did they speculate as to the possibility of their own destruction at the hands of the natives of Karolin; they had little imagination and big belief in Rantan, and, having talked for a while and chosen a man to keep watch, they dived below. Then dark came and the stars.

Kanoa was the man chosen, a pure Polynesian from Vana Vana, not more than eighteen, slim and straight as a dart, and with lustrous eyes that shone now in the dusk as he turned them on Le Moan, the only living creature on deck beside himself.

He had been watching Le Moan for days, for weeks, with an ever-increasing interest. She had repelled him at first despite her beauty, and owing to her strange ways. He had never seen a girl like her at Vana Vana nor at Tuta Kotu, and to his simple mind, she was something more than a girl, maybe something less, a creature that loved to brood alone and live alone, perchance spirit; who could tell, for it was well known at Vana Vana that spirits of men and women were sometimes met with at sea on desolate reefs and atolls, ghosts of drowned people who would even light fires to attract ships and canoes and be taken off just as Le Moan had been taken off by Pete'son, and who always brought disaster to the ship or canoe foolish enough to rescue them.

Sru had kicked him for speaking like this in the foc'sle. After Pete'son had been left behind at Levua, supposedly killed by Tahaku and his followers, Kanoa, leaning on his side in his bunk and pipe in mouth had said: "It is the girl or she that looks like a girl but is maybe the spirit of some woman lost at sea. She was alone on that island and Pete'son brought her on board and now, look—what has become of Pete'son?" Upon which Sru had pulled him out of his bunk and kicked him. All the same Kanoa's mind did not leave hold of the idea. He was convinced that there was more to come in the way of disaster, and now, look, Sru gone and three men with him!

But Kanoa was only eighteen and Le Moan for all her dark beauty and brooding ways and mysterious habits was, at all events, fashioned in the form of a girl, and once in a roll of the ship Le Moan slipping on the spray-wet deck would have fallen, only for Kanoa who caught her, almost naked as she was, in his arms, and she was delicious.

Ghost or not there began to grow in him a desire for her that was held in check only by his fear of her. A strange condition of mind brought about by the conflict of two passions.

Tonight close to her on the deserted deck, the warm air bringing her perfume to him and her body outlined against the starlit lagoon, he was only prevented from seizing her in his arms by the thought of Sru and his companions dead on the reef over there; dead as Pete'son, dead as he—Kanoa—might be tomorrow, and through the wiles of this girl so like a spirit, this spirit so like a girl.

He felt like a man swimming against the warm current that sweeps round the shoulder of Haraikai, swimming bravely and seeming to make good way, yet all the time being swept steadily out to sea to drown and die.

Suddenly—and just as he was about to fling out his hands, seize her and capture her in a burning embrace, mouth to mouth, breast to breast, and arms locked round her body—suddenly the initiative was taken from him and Le Moan, gliding up to him, placed a hand upon his shoulder.

Next moment she had pressed him down to the deck and he was squatting opposite to her, almost knee to knee, love for the moment forgotten.

Forgotten even though, leaning forward and placing her hand on his shoulder, she brought her face almost in touch with his.

"Kanoa," said Le Moan, in a voice just audible to him above the rumble of the reef, "Sru and the men who were with him have been slain by Rantan, and the big red man, not by the men of Karolin. Tomorrow you will die, I heard him say so to the big man, you and Timau and Tahuku and Poni and Nauta and Tirai." She told this lie with steady eyes fixed upon him, eyes that saw nothing but Taori, the man whose life she was trying to save. No wonder that love dropped out of the heart of Kanoa and that the sweat showed on his face in the starlight. It was the first time that she had spoken to him more than a word or two, and what she said in that swift clear whisper passed through him like a sword. He believed her. His fear of her was the basis of his belief. He was listening to the voice of a spirit, not the voice of a girl.

He who a moment ago had been filled with passionate desire, felt now that he was sitting knee to knee with Death.

Such was the conviction carried by her words and voice that he would have risen up and run away and hidden, only that he could not move.

"Unless," said Le Moan, "we strike them tonight, tomorrow we will all be killed."

Kanoa's teeth began to chatter. His frightened mind flew back to Vana Vana and the happy days of his youth. He wished that he had never embarked on this voyage that had led him to so many strange passes. Strike them! It was easy to say that, but who would dare to strike Ra'tan?

He was seated facing aft and he could see the vague glow of the saloon skylight golden in the silver of the star-shine. Down below there in the lamplight Ra'tan and the red bearded one were no doubt talking and making their plans. Strike them! That was easily said.

Then, all at once, he stopped shivering and his teeth came together with a click. The light from the saloon had gone out.

He touched Le Moan and told her and she turned her head to the long sweep of the deck, empty, and deserted by the vanished light. It was as though the power of the after guard had suffered eclipse. Rantan and the other would be soon asleep, if they were not asleep now, helpless and at the mercy of the man who would be brave enough to strike.

Le Moan turned again and seizing Kanoa by the shoulder whispered close to his ear.

"Go," said she; "tell the others what I have said, bring them up, softly, Mayana, softly so that *they* may not hear, they need lift no hand in the business. I will strike; go!"

He rose up and passed towards the foc'sle hatch whilst Le Moan, going into the galley, fetched something she had hidden there—the head of the spear which she had broken off from the shaft, the spear Carlin had brought on board as a trophy, and the snap of which he had heard as he lay in his bunk whilst Rantan had been lighting his pipe.

She sat down on the deck with the deadly thing on her knee, poisoned with argora. A scratch from it would be sufficient to destroy life almost instantaneously, and as she sat brooding and waiting, her eyes saw neither the deck nor the starlight, but the vision of a sunlit beach and a form, Taori. Taori for whom she would have destroyed the world.

The sea spoke on the great reef loud to windward, low to leeward; you could hear within the long rumble and roar of the nearby breakers the diminuendo of the rollers that smoked beneath the stars, ringing with a forty-mile mist the placid ocean of the lagoon.

The moon was rising. She could see the gleam of its light on the binnacle where the Godling lived that had always pointed away from Karolin, on the port rail and on the brass-work of the skylight. Then, roused by a sound soft as the sifting of leaves on a lawn, she turned and behind her the deck was crowded.

The crew had come on deck led by Kanoa, and the stern of the schooner swinging towards the break with the tide, the level light of the moon was on their faces.

V

NIGHT, DEATH AND PASSION

She made them sit down and they sat in a ring on the deck, she taking her place in the middle.

Then she talked to them respecting what she had already told to Kanoa, telling them also that the men of Karolin were not enemies but friends, that Rantan and the red-bearded man though fair-spoken were indeed devils in disguise, that they had killed many of the men of Karolin, killed Sru and his companions and intended on the morrow to kill Kanoa and the rest. And they sat listening to her as children listen to the tales about ogres—believing, bewildered, terrified, not knowing what to do.

These men were not cowards; under circumstances known and understood they were brave, weather could not frighten them nor war against kindred races, but the white man was a different thing and Rantan they feared even more than Carlin.

They would not move a hand in this matter of striking at them. It would be better to take the boat and land on the reef and trust to the men of Karolin if they were trustworthy as Le Moan had reported.

Poni, the biggest and strongest of them, said this and the others nodded their heads in approval, and Le Moan laughed; she knew them and told them so, told them that as she had saved them by overhearing Rantan's plans, she would save them now, that they had nothing to do but wait and watch and prepare their minds for friendship with her people when she had finished what she intended to do.

Then she rose up.

As she stood with the moonlight full on her, a voice broke the silence of the night. It came from the saloon hatchway, a voice sudden, chattering, complaining and ceasing all at once as if cut off by a closed door. They knew what it was, the voice of a man talking in his sleep. Carlin on his back and seized by nightmare had cried out, half awakened, turned and fallen asleep again.

The group seated on the deck, after a momentary movement, resumed their positions. There is something so distinctive in the voice of a sleep-talker that the sound, after the first momentary flutter caused by it, brought assurance. Then, prepared at any moment to make a dash for the boat, they sat, the palms of their hands flat on the deck and their eyes following Le Moan, now gliding towards the hatch, the spear head in her left hand, her right hand touching the port rail as she went.

At the hatch she paused to listen. She could hear the reef, and on its sonorous murmur like a tiny silver thread of sound the trickle of the tide on the planking of the schooner, and from the dark pit of the stairway leading to the saloon another sound, the breathing of men asleep.

She had never been below. That stairway, even in daylight, had always filled her with fear, the fear of the unknown, the dread of a trap, the claustrophobia of one always used to open spaces.

Lit by the day it frightened her, in its black darkness it appalled her; yet she had to go down, for the life of Taori lay at the bottom of that pit to be saved by her hands and hers alone.

Kanoa, amongst the others, sat watching. The mind of Kanoa so filled with fear when she told him that his death was imminent, the mind of Kanoa that had lusted for her, the mind of this child of eighteen to whom light and laughter had been life and thought, a thing of the moment, was no longer the same mind.

The great heroism he was watching, this attempt to save him and the others, had awakened in him something perhaps of the past, ancestors who had fought, done great deeds and suffered—who knows—but there came to him an elation such as he had felt in the movements of the dance and at the sound of music. Rising and evading Poni who clutched at his leg to hold him back, he came to the rail, stood for a moment as Le Moan vanished from sight and then swiftfooted but silent as a shadow, glided to the saloon hatch and stood listening.

Holding the polished banister rail, and moving cautiously, step by step, Le Moan descended, the spear head in her left hand. As she came, a waft from the cabin rose to meet her in the darkness—an odour of humanity and stale tobacco smoke, bunk-bedding and bilge.

It met her like an evil ghost, it grappled with her and tried to drive her back; used as she was to the fresh sea air, able to scent rain on the wind and change of weather, this odour checked her for a moment, repelled her, held her and then lost its power; her will had conquered it. She reached the foot of the stairs and before her now lay the open doorway of the cabin, a pale oblong beyond which lay a picture.

The table with the swinging lamp above it, the bunks on either side where the sleeping men lay, clothes cast on the floor, all lit by the moon-gleams through the skylight and portholes.

HENRY DE VERE STACPOOLE

From the bunk on the right hung an arm. It was Carlin's; she knew it by its size. She moved towards it, paused, looked up and stood rigid.

Above Carlin, now on the ceiling, now on the wall, something moved and danced; a great silver butterfly, now at rest, now in flight, shifting here and there, poising with tremulous wings.

It was a water shimmer from the moonlit lagoon entering through a porthole, a ghost of light; it held her only for a moment, the next she had seized the hand of the sleeper and driven the spear point into the arm. Almost on the cry of the stricken man, something sprang across the table of the cabin, seized Le Moan by the throat and flung her on her side. It was Rantan.

Up above Kanoa, standing by the opening of the hatch, listening. The reef spoke and the water trickled on the planking, but from below there came no sound. Moments passed and then, sharp and cutting the silence like a knife came a cry, a shout, and the sound of a furious struggle. Then, fear flown and filled with a fury new as life to the newborn, Kanoa plunged down into the darkness, missed his footing, fell, rose half stunned and dashed into the cabin.

Carlin, naked, was lying on his face on the floor, dead or dying; Rantan, naked, was at death grips with Le Moan. She had risen by a supreme effort, but he had got her against the table, flung her on it and was now holding her down, his knee on her thigh, his hands on her throat, his head flung back, the flexor muscles of his forearms rigid, crushing her, breaking her, choking the life out of her, till Kanoa sprang.

Sprang like a tiger, lighting on the table and then in a flash on to Rantan's back, breaking his grip with the impact and freeing Le Moan. He had got the throat hold from behind, his knees had seized Rantan's body and he was riding him like a horse. The attacked man, whooping and choking, tried to hit backwards, flung up his arms, rose straight, tottered and crashed, but still the attacker clung, clung as they rolled on the floor, clung till all movement ceased.

It was over.

The silver butterfly still danced merrily on the ceiling and the sound of the reef came through the skylight, slumbrous and indifferent, but other sound or movement there was none till Le Moan, stretched still on the table, turned, raised herself on her elbow and understood. Then she dropped on to the floor. Rantan lay half on top of Carlin and Kanoa lay by Rantan.

Kanoa's grip had relaxed and he seemed asleep. He roused as the girl touched him; the fury and wild excitement had passed, he seemed dazed; then recovering himself he sat up, then he rose to his feet. As he rose Rantan moved slightly, he was not dead and Le Moan kneeling on the body of Carlin seized the sheet that was hanging from the bunk, dragged it towards her and handed it to Kanoa.

"Bind him," said Le Moan, "he is not dead, let him be for my people to deal with him as they deal with the dog-fish."

As they bound him from the shoulders to the hands a voice came from above. It was the voice of Poni who had come to listen and who heard Le Moan's voice and words.

"Kanoa," cried Poni, "what is going on below there?"

"Coward!" cried Le Moan, "come and see. Come and help now that the work is done."

"Ay," said Kanoa the valorous, "come and help now that the work is done."

Then, kneeling by the bound figure of Rantan, he gazed on the girl, consuming her with his eyes, rapturous, and unknowing that the work had been done for Taori.

Taori, beside whom, for Le Moan, all other men were shadows, moving yet lifeless as the moon-born butterfly still dancing above the corpse of Carlin.

VI

Morning

When the firing had ceased and the boat had returned to the ship the wretched people hiding amongst the mammee apple had come out and grouped themselves around Aioma and Taori. Taori had saved them for the moment by his act in swimming out to attack the boat; he was no longer their chief, but their god, and yet some instinctive knowledge of the wickedness of man and of the tenacity and power of the white men told them that all was not over.

Amongst them as they waited whilst Aioma and Katafa distributed food, sat two women, Nanu and Ona, each with a dead child clasped in her arms. The child of Nanu had been killed instantaneously by a bullet that had pierced its neck and the arm of its mother. Ona's child, pierced in its body, had died slowly, bleeding its life away and wailing as it bled.

These two women, high cheeked, frizzy-headed and of the old fierce Melanesian stock which formed the backbone and hitting force of Karolin, were strange to watch as they sat nursing their dead, speechless, passionless, heedless of food or drink or what might happen. The others ate, too paralysed by the events of the day to prepare food for themselves, they yet took what was given to them with avidity, then, when dark came, they crept back into the bushes to sleep, whilst Dick, leaving Katafa in charge of Aioma, left the trees and under cover of the darkness came along the beach past the bodies, over which the birds were still at work, until he was level with the schooner.

She showed no lights on deck, no sign of life but the two tiny dim golden discs of the cabin portholes.

Taking his seat on a weather-worn piece of coral, he sat watching her. Forward, close to the foc'sle head, he saw now two forms, Le Moan and Kanoa; they drew together, then they vanished, the deck now seemed deserted, but he continued to watch. Already in his mind he foresaw vaguely the plan of Rantan. Tomorrow they would not use the boat, they would move the schooner, bring her opposite the village and then with those terrible things that could speak so loudly and hit so far they would begin again—and where could the people go? The forty-mile reef would be no protection; away from the trees and the puraka patches the people would starve, they would have no water. The people were tied to the village.

He sat with his chin on his clenched fists staring at the schooner and the two evil golden eyes that were staring him back like the eyes of a beast.

If only a single canoe had been left he would have paddled off and, with Aioma and maybe another for help, would have attacked, but the canoes were gone—and the dinghy.

Then as he sat helpless, with hatred and the fury of hell in his heart, the golden eyes vanished. Rantan had put out the light.

With the rising moon he saw as in a glass, darkly, little by little and bit by bit, the tragedy we have seen in full. He saw the grouping of the foc'sle hands as they came up from below, he saw them disappear as they sat on deck. Then he saw the figure of Le Moan, her halt at the saloon hatch and the following of Kanoa, he heard the scream of the stricken Carlin.

Lastly he saw the crowding of the hands aft, Carlin's body being dragged on deck and cast overboard into a lather of moonshine and phosphorus, and something white carried shoulder high to forward of the galley where it was laid on deck.

Then after a few moments lights began to break out, lanterns moved on the deck, the portholes broke alive again and again were blotted out as the cabin lamp lit and taken from its attachments was carried on deck and swung from the ratlins of the main for decorative purposes. The moon gave all the light that any man in his sober senses could want, but the crew of the schooner were not sober, they were drunk with the excitement of the business, and though nominally free men they felt as slaves feel when their bonds are removed. Besides, Rantan and Carlin had plotted to kill them as they had killed Sru and the others. On top of that there was a bottle of ginger wine. It had been stored in the medicine locker—Peterson, like many other seamen, had medical fancies of his own and he believed this stuff to be a specific for the colic. It had escaped Carlin's attention, but Poni, who acted as steward, had sniffed at it, tasted it and found it good.

It was served out in a tin cup.

Then, across the water came the sound of voices, the twanging of a native fiddle, and now the whoop-whoop of dancers in the hula dance songs, laughter against which came the thunder of the moonlit sea on the outer beach and an occasional cry from the gulls at their food.

Dick, rising, made back towards the trees; his heart felt easier. Without knowing what had occurred, he still knew that something had happened to divide his enemies, that they had quarrelled, and that one had been killed; that, with Sru and his companions, made five gone since the schooner had dropped anchor.

Lying down beside Katafa, whilst Taiepu kept watch, he fell asleep.

At dawn Taiepu, shouting like a gull, came racing through the trees whilst the bushes gave up their people. They came crowding out on the beach to eastward of the trees and there, sure enough, was Le Moan, the schooner against the blaze at the Gates of Morning, and the boat hanging a hundred yards off shore.

Kneeling on the sands before Taori, glancing sometimes up into his face, swiftly, as one glances at the sun, Le Moan told her tale whilst the sun itself now fully risen blazed upon the man before her.

Dick listened, gathered from the artless story the sacrifices she had made at first, the heroism she had shown to the last, but nothing of her real motive, nothing of the passion that came nigh to crushing her as Katafa, catching her in her arms, and, pressing her lips on her forehead, led her away tenderly as a sister to the shelter of the trees.

Then the mob, true to itself and forgetting their saviour, turning, raced along the sands, boys, women and children, till they got level with the waiting boat shouting welcome to the newcomers.

Poni in the stern sheets rose and waved his arms, the boat driven by a few strokes reached the beach and next moment the crew of the *Kermadec* and the people of Karolin were fraternizing—embracing one another like long-lost relatives.

And now a strange thing happened.

Dick, who stood watching all this, deposed for a moment as chief men are sometimes temporarily deposed and forgotten in moments of great national heart movements, saw in the boat, the naked, bound figure of Rantan lying on the bottom boards.

He came closer and the eyes of Rantan, which were open, met the eyes of Taori.

Rantan was a white man.

There was no appeal in the eyes of Rantan—he who knew the Islands so well knew that his number was up; he gazed at the golden brown figure of Taori, gazed at that face so strange for a kanaka, yet so truly the face of an islander, gazed as a white man upon a native.

For a moment it was as though race gazed upon kindred race disowning it, not seeing it, mistaking it for an alien and lower race and from deep in the mind of Dick vague and phantom-like rose trouble.

He did not know that he himself was a white man, blood brother of the man in the boat. He knew nothing, yet he felt trouble. He turned to Aioma.

"Will he die?"

"Ay, most surely will he die," said the old fellow with a chuckle. "Will the dog-fish not die when he is caught? He who killed the canoes, the children, is it not just that he should die?"

Dick inclined his head without speaking. He turned to where Nanu and the other woman were standing, waiting, terrible, with their dead children still clasped in their arms.

"It is just," said he, "see to it, Aioma," and turning without another glance at the boat he walked away, past the shattered canoes, past the half-picked bones, through the sunlight, towards the trees.

Aioma, no longer himself, but something more evil, came towards the boat making little bird-like noises, rubbing his shrivelled hands together, stroking his thighs.

The tide was just at full ebb, the old ledge where the victims of Nanawa were staked out in past times for the sharks to eat was uncovered and only waiting for a victim. It lay halfway between the village and the reef break and in old times one might have known when an execution was to take place by the fins of the tiger sharks cruising around it. This morning there were no sharks visible.

Rantan was reserved for a worse fate; for, as Aioma, standing by the boat, called on the people to take their vengeance, the woman Nanu, still holding her dead child in her arms stepped up to him followed by Ona.

"He is ours," said Nanu.

Aioma turned on her like a savage old dog—he was about to push her back amongst the crowd when Ona advanced a step.

"He is ours," said Ona, glancing at the form in the boat as though it were a parcel she was claiming, whilst the crowd, reaching to the woods, broke in, speaking almost with one voice.

"He is theirs, he has slain their children, let them have him for a child."

"So be it," said Aioma, too much of a diplomat to oppose the mob on a matter of sentiment, and curious as to what gory form of vengeance the women would adopt. "So be it, and now what will you do with him?"

"We will take him to the southern beach with us. We alone," said Nanu.

HENRY DE VERE STACPOOLE

"We would be alone with him," said Ona, shifting her dead child from her right to her left arm as one might shift a parcel.

"But how will you take him?" asked the old man.

"In a canoe," said Nanu.

"Then go and build it," said the canoe-builder. "What foolishness is this, for well you know the canoes are broken."

"Aioma," said Nanu, "there is one little canoe which is yet whole, it lies in the further canoe-house, so far in that it has been forgotten; it belonged to my man, the father of my child, he who went with the others but did not return. I have never spoken of it and no one has seen it, for no one goes into the canoe-houses now that the great canoes are gone."

"Then let it be fetched," said Aioma. He stood whilst a dozen of the crowd broke away and racing towards the trees disappeared in the direction of the canoe-houses. Presently the canoe, a fishing outrigger, showed on the water of the lagoon, two boys at the paddles. They beached it close to the boat, the dead children were lashed to the gratings with strips of coconut sennit, Rantan, raised by half a dozen pairs of hands, was lifted and placed in the bottom of the little craft, and the women, pushing off, got on board, and raised the sail.

The steering paddle flashed and the crowd stood watching as the canoe grew less on the surface of the water, less and less, making for the southern beach, till now it was no larger than a midge in the lagoon dazzle that, striking back at the sun, roofed Karolin with a forty-mile dome of radiance.

VII

THE VISION

N ow when Katafa led Le Moan away into the shelter of the trees,
Le Moan, with the kiss of Katafa warm upon her forehead, knew
nothing, nothing of the fact that Katafa was Taori's, the dream and
treasure of his life, beside whom all other living things were shadows.

And Katafa knew nothing, nothing of the fact that Taori was Le
Moan's—was Le Moan; for Le Moan had so dreamed him into herself
that the vision of him had become part of herself inseparable forever.

Ringed and ringed with ignorance, ignorance of their own race,
and the affinity between them, of the fact that they and Taori formed
amongst the people of Karolin a little colony alien in blood and soul,
of the fact that Taori was their common desire, they went between the
trees, Katafa leading the way towards the house of Uta Matu, above
which Nan on his pole still grinned towards the schooner, grinned
without nodding, maybe because the wind that had moved him had
ceased.

Katafa, taking the sleeping mat used by her and Taori, spread it on
the floor of the house, then she offered food, but Le Moan refused, she
only wanted sleep. For nights she had not slept and the kiss that Katafa
again pressed upon her brow seemed to her the kiss of a phantom in a
dream as she sank down and died to the world on the bed of the lover
who knew nothing of her love.

It was still morning.

Outside in the blazing sun the people of Karolin went about their
business, mending the wall of the house that had been broken, preparing
food for the newcomers, rejoicing in the new life that had come back
to them. Whilst in the lagoon the anchored schooner swung to her
moorings, deserted and without sign of life, for Dick had decided that
no one should board her till he and Aioma led the way, that is till the
morrow, for there were many things to be attended to first.

Le Moan had brought him not only a ship, but six full-grown men,
a priceless gift if the men were to be trusted.

Aioma, who had held off from the business of fraternizing, watching
the newcomers with a critical eye, believed that they were good men.

"But wait," said Aioma, "till they are fed, till they have rested and slept amongst us; a good-looking coconut is sometimes rotten at the core, but these I believe to be good men even as Le Moan has said; but tonight will tell."

At dusk he came to Taori, happy. Each of the new men had taken a wife; incidentally, in the next few days each of the newcomers, with one exception, had taken from four to six wives.

"Each has a woman," said the direct Aioma. "We are sure of them now, they are in the mammee apple, all except one who is very young and who says that he has no heart for women."

He spoke of Kanoa. Kanoa brooding alone by the water's edge, sick with love and desire. Love that was even greater than desire, for the deed of Le Moan that had stirred in him the ghosts of his ancestors, had raised the soul of Kanoa beyond the flesh where hitherto it had been tangled and blind.

Meanwhile Le Moan slept. Slept whilst the dusk rose and the stars came out, slept till the moon high against the milky way pierced the house of Uta Matu with her shafts.

Then sleep fell from her gradually and turning on her elbow she saw the moon rays shining through the canes of the wall, the little ships ghostly on their shelves and through the doorway the wonderful world of moonlit reef and sea.

Nothing broke the stillness of the night but the surf of the reef and a gentle wind that stirred the palm fronds with a faint pattering rainy sound and passed away across the mammee apple where men and women lay embraced, who the night before had not known even of each other's existence.

Before the doorway, sheltered from the moon by a tree shadow, all but their feet that showed fully in the light, two forms lay stretched on a mat—Taori and Katafa. They had given up their house to the saviour of Karolin, taken a mat from one of the women's houses, and fallen asleep with only the tree for shelter. Le Moan, not recognizing them, still dazed with sleep, rose, came to the doorway and looked down.

Then she knew.

Taori's head was pillowed on Katafa's shoulder, her arm was around his neck, his arm across her body.

VIII

The Cassi Flowers

If the sea had risen above the reef destroying the village and sweeping the population of Karolin to ruin whilst leaving her untouched, Le Moan would have stood as she stood now, unmoved before the inevitable and the accomplished.

Her world lay around her in ruins and the destroyers lay before her asleep.

She had feared death and dreaded separation, but she had never dreamed of this—for Taori, in her mind, had always stood alone as the sun stands alone in the sky.

A spear stood against the tree bole and the pitiless hand that had killed Carlin could have seized it and plunged it into the heart of Katafa, but if the sea had destroyed her world as this girl had destroyed it, would she have cast a spear at the sea? The thing was done, accomplished, of old time. Her woman's instinct told her that.

Done and accomplished, without any knowledge of her, in a world from which she had been excluded by fate.

Moving from the doorway she passed them, almost touching their feet. To right and left of her lay the tumbling sea and the lit lagoon, before her the great white road of the beaches and the reef. She followed the leading of this road with little more volition than the wind-blown leaf or the drifting weed; with only one desire, to be alone.

It led to the great trees where the canoe-builders had been at work. Here across the coral lay the trunks felled by Aioma, filling the air with the fragrance of new-cut wood. One already had been partly shaped and hollowed, and resting on it for a moment, Le Moan followed its curves with her eyes, felt the ax marks with her hand, took in every detail of the work, saw it as, with outrigger affixed and sail spread to the wind, it would take the sea, sometime—sometime—sometime.

The ceaseless breakers casting their spindrift beneath the moon lulled her mind for a moment till trees, canoe, reef and sea all faded and dissolved in a world of sound, a voice-world through which came the chanting of stricken coral and, at last, pictures of the wind-blown southern beach.

The southern beach, sunlit and gull-flown, a beached canoe, a form—Taori.

It was now and now only that the pain came, piercing soul and rending body, crushing her and breaking her till she fell on the coral, her face buried in her arms, as though cast there by the sea whose eternal thunder filled the night.

The night wind moved her hair. It was blowing from the village and as it came it brought with it a vague whisper from the bushes and trees and now and again a faint perfume of cassi. Perfume, like music, is a voice speaking a language we have forgotten, telling tales we half understand, soothing us now with dreams, raising us now to action.

The cassi flowers were speaking to Le Moan. After a long, long while she moved, raised her head and, leaning on her elbow, seemed to listen.

Close to her was a pond in the coral—a rock pool filled with fresh water such as existed on the southern beach and a fellow of which lay in the village close to the house of Uta Matu.

Dragging herself towards it she leaned on her arms and looked deep down into the water just as she had been looking into the pool that day when raising her eyes she found herself first face to face with Taori.

The cassi flowers were speaking to Le Moan, their perfume followed her mind as it sank like a diver into the pool's moonlit, crystal heart. Their voices said to her:

"Taori is not dead. Whilst he lives do not despair, for who can take his image from you and what woman's love can equal yours? Peace, Le Moan. Watch and wait."

Presently she arose, returning by the way she came. She drew towards the house of Uta Matu and passed the figures on the mat without glancing at them. Then in the house she lay down with her face to the wall. When the dawn aroused Katafa, Le Moan had not moved; one might have fancied her asleep.

IX

Vengeance

Rantan, when they cast him in the fishing canoe, could see nothing but the roughly shaped sides, bright here and there where the scale of a palu had stuck and dried, the after outrigger pole, the blue sky above the gunnel and the heads of the crowd by the waterside.

By raising himself a little he might have glimpsed the two dead children tied to the outrigger gratings, but he could not raise himself, nor had he any desire to do so.

He knew the islands, he had heard what passed between Aioma and the women, and as they carried him from the boat to the canoe, he had seen the dead children tied on the gratings. What his fate was to be at the hands of Ona and Nanu he could not tell, nor did he try to imagine it.

All being ready, the stem of the canoe left the beach, the two women scrambling on board as it was waterborne. Nanu sat aft and Ona forward, trampling on Rantan's body with her naked feet as she got there. The paddles splashed and the spray came inboard striking Rantan on the face, but he did not mind; neither did he mind the heat of the steadily rising sun, nor the heel of Ona as she dropped her paddle for a moment and raised the sail.

Sometimes he closed his eyes to shut out the sight of Nanu, who was steering, her eyes fixed on the sail; sometimes on the beach ahead, never or scarcely ever on Rantan.

Sometimes he could hear Ona's voice. She was just behind his head holding on to the mast and trimming the canoe by moving now to the left or right—her voice came calling out some directions to the other and then sharp as the voice of Ona came the cry of a seagull that flew with them for a moment, inspecting the dead children on the gratings till the flashing paddle and the shouts of Nanu drove it away.

And now as the sun grew hotter, a vague odour of corruption filled the air, passed away with the back draught from the sail yet returned again, whilst the murmur of the northern beach that had died down behind them became merged in the wash of the waves on the southern coral.

HENRY DE VERE STACPOOLE

Then as the place of their revenge drew close to them and they could see the deserted shacks, the long line of empty beach and the coconut trees in their separate groups, Nanu seemed to awake to the presence of Rantan. She glanced at him and laughed, and steering all the time, with side flashes of the paddle pointed him out to Ona whose laughter came from behind him, shrill, sharp and done with in a moment.

Truly Rantan wished that he had never embarked on this voyage, never seen Peterson, never left him for dead away there on Levua; bitterly did he repent his temerity in coming into Karolin lagoon and his stupidity in trying to shoot it up.

Sometimes, long ago, he had amused himself by imagining what might be the worst fate of a man at sea, shipwreck, slow starvation, death from thirst, from sharks, from fire. He had never imagined anything like his present position, never imagined himself in the hands of two women of the Islands, whose children he had been instrumental in murdering, two women who were taking him off to a desolate beach to do with him as they pleased. He could tell the approach of the beach by the face of Nanu and the outcries of Ona. Sometimes Ona would give his body a kick to emphasize what she was saying, which was Greek to Rantan. So sharp was her voice, so run together the words, that her speech was like a sword inscribed with unintelligible threats.

Now Nanu was half standing up, Ona was hauling the sail, the paddles were flashing, the sands close. They brought the stem of the canoe on to the shelving sand, and, on the bump and shudder, dropping their paddles, they jumped clear, seized gunnel and out-rigger and beached her high and dry.

Then seizing their victim by the feet and the shoulders, they lifted him from the canoe and threw him on to the sand. He fell on his face, they turned him on his back and then left him, running about here and there and making preparations for their work.

The tide was running out and the wind, that had slacked to due west, bent the coco palms and brought up from all along the beach the silky whisper of the sands, the rumour of twenty miles of sea beating on the southern coral and the smell of sun-smitten sea-weeds and emptying rock pools.

Rantan, who had closed his eyes, opened them, and turning his head slightly, watched the women; Nanu who was collecting bits of stick and wood to light a fire and Ona who was collecting oyster shells. There were many oyster shells lying about on the beach and Ona, as she went, picked and chose, taking only the flat shells and testing their edges with her thumb.

Rantan knew, and a shudder went through him as he watched her carrying them and placing them in a little heap by the place where Nanu was building her fire.

A big brown bird with curved beak and bright eyes sweeping in the air above them would curve and drift on the wind and return, making a swoop towards the beached canoe and the objects on the outrigger gratings, and the women, busy at their work, would shout at the bird and sometimes threaten it with a paddle which Ona ran and fetched from the canoe. Not till vengeance had been assured would the dead children be cast to the sharks. The shark was the grave and burial-ground of Karolin.

When everything was ready they turned from the fire and came running across the sand to their victim.

Rantan, lying on his back with eyes closed and mouth open, had ceased to breathe.

Never looked man more dead than Rantan, and Ona, dropping on her knees beside him with a cry, turned him on one side, turned him back, cried out to Nanu who dashed off to the fire, seized a piece of burning stick, rushed back with it and pressed the red hot point of it against his foot. Rantan did not move.

Then furious, filling the air with their cries, with only one idea, to rub him and pound him and to bring back the precious life that had escaped or was escaping them, they began to strip him of his bonds, tearing off the coconut sennit strips, the sheet, unrolling him like a mummy from its bandages, till he lay naked beneath the sun—a corpse that suddenly sprang to life with a yell, bounded to its feet, seized the paddle and flung itself on Nanu, felling her with a smashing blow on the neck, turned and pursuing Ona chased her as she ran this way and that like a frightened duck.

Few men had ever seen Rantan. The silent, quiet, sunburnt man of ordinary times was not Rantan. This was Rantan, this mad figure yelling hatred, radiating revenge, mad to kill.

Rantan robbed of his pearl lagoon, of his ship, of his prospect of wealth, ease, wine and women—by kanakas; Rantan whom kanakas had bound with a sheet and dumped into a canoe; Rantan whom two kanaka women—women!—women, mind you—had trodden on, and whom they had been preparing to scrape to death slowly inch by inch with oyster shells, and burn bit by bit with hot sticks.

This was the real Rantan raised to his nth power by injuries, insults, and the escape from a terrible death.

Ona dashed for the canoe, maybe with some blind idea to get hold of the other paddle to defend herself with, but he had the speed of her and headed her off; she made for the rough coral of the outer beach but he headed her off; time and again he could have closed with her and killed her, but the sight of her frizzy head, her face, her figure, and the fact that she was a woman, filled him with a counter rage that spared her for the moment. He could have chased her forever, killing her a thousand times in his mind, had his strength been equal to his hatred; but he could not chase her forever, and, suddenly, with a smashing blow he brought her to ground, beat the life out of her and stood gasping, satiated and satisfied.

Only for a moment. The sight of Nanu lying where he had felled her brought him running. She had fallen near the heap of oyster shells, the fire that she had built was still burning, the stick which she had pressed against his foot was close to her. She had recovered consciousness and as she lay, her eyes wide open, she saw him stand above her, the paddle uplifted, and that was the last thing she saw in this world.

He came down to the water's edge and sat, squatting, the paddle beside him and his eyes fixed away over the water to where the schooner was visible, a toy ship no larger than the model of the *Rarotonga*, swinging to the outgoing tide.

Beyond the schooner the trees that hid the village were just visible.

He was free, free for the moment, but still in the trap of the lagoon.

Free, but stripped of everything; absolutely naked, without even shoes.

He was thinking in pictures; pictures now vague, now clear ran through his mind, the shooting up of the lagoon, the figure of Dick swimming off towards him and Carlin as they were firing from the boat, the fight in the cabin, the killing of Carlin—and again Dick.

Dick as he had come and stood looking at him (Rantan) as he lay bound and helpless. His hatred of the kanakas and the whole business seemed focussed in Dick, for in that bright figure and noble face lay expressed the antithesis of himself, something that he could not despise as he despised Sru, the Karolin people, even Carlin.

He loathed this creature whom he had only seen twice and to whom he had never spoken—loathed him as hell loathes heaven.

Then Dick dropped from his mind.

He was still in the trap of the lagoon. He turned his head to where behind him on the sands lay the two dead women, then he turned his eyes to the beached canoe where lay the two dead children strapped to the gratings. The waves spoke and the wind on the sands, and the bo'sun bird returning with a mate swept by, casting its shadow close to him.

Rantan shouted and picking up the paddle threatened the bird just as the women had done, then he sprang to his feet.

He must get out, get out with the canoe, clear off before the kanakas had any chance of coming across. They had no canoes, but they had the ship's boats and if they came and caught him, it would be death; he could get drinking nuts from the trees, but first he must untie those cursed children from the gratings. He turned towards the canoe and as he turned something caught his eye away across the water.

The merry west wind had blown out a bunt of the schooner's hastily stowed canvas in a white flicker against the blue. Were they getting sail on the schooner?

He turned and ran towards the trees. He could climb like a monkey, and heedless of everything but drinking nuts and pandanus drupes, he set to work, collecting them. A mat lay doubled up near one of the deserted shacks; he used it as a basket and between the trees and the canoe he ran and ran, sweating, with scarcely a glance across the water—his only idea the thirst and hunger of the sea which he had to face, the terror of torture and death that lay behind him. There was a huge fig tree, the only one on Karolin, and a tree bearing an unknown fruit in form and colour like a lemon. He raided them, tearing branches down and stripping the fruit off. Before his last journey to the canoe he flung himself down by the little well, the same into which Le Moan had been gazing when she first saw Taori, and drank and drank—raising his head only to drink again.

Reaching the canoe for the last time he threw the fruit in and took a glance across the water to the schooner. The wind had taken advantage of the clumsy and careless work of the crew and the size of the bunt had increased. In his right senses he would have known the truth, but terror had him by the shoulder and seizing the gunnel he began to drive the canoe into the water. The falling tide had left her almost dry, the outrigger interfered with his efforts, getting half buried in the sand. He could not push her out and at the same time keep her level with the outrigger lifting. He had to run from side to side pushing and striving, till at last the idea came to him to spread the mat under the outrigger.

That made things easier. He had her now nearly waterborne; throwing in the paddle he prepared to send her out with a last great push, and, running through the shallow water, scramble on board.

Such was the state of his mind he had not recognized that the bodies of the two babies tied to the gratings were a main cause in the tilting of the canoe to port and his difficulty in keeping her on a level keel; nor did he now, but he recognized that he could not put to sea with those terrible bodies tied to him.

He set to work to untie them, but Nanu and Ona, as though previsioning this business, had done their work truly and well—the spray and the sun had shrunk the coconut sennit bindings and the knots were hard as bits of oak. He had no knife, and his hands were shaking and his fingers without power.

A gull swooped down as if to help him and he struck at it with his fist; the sweat poured from him and his knees were beginning to knock together.

The tide was still falling, threatening to leave the canoe dry again; he recognized that and, leaving the bodies untied, raced round to the starboard side, seized the gunnel and pushed her out. On board he paddled kneeling, and using the paddle now on one side, now on the other; making straight out, the lose sail flapping above him, his knees wet with crushed pandanus drupes, gulls following him swooping down and clanging off on the wind.

Then, far enough out, he gave the sail to the breeze that was blowing steady for the break. He was free, nobody could stop him now. Wind and tide were with him, so were the lagoon sharks, who guessed what was tied to the gratings and the gulls who saw.

A royal escort of gulls snowed the air above the flashing paddle and the bellying sail as the canoe, driving past the piers of the opening took the sea and the outer swell, steering dead before the wind for the east.

Little by little the gulls fell astern, gave up the chase, swept back towards Karolin, leaving the man and the dead children and the canoe to the blue sea and the wind that swept it.

Rantan steered. He was used to the handling of a canoe and he knew that, alone as he was, he could do nothing but just keep the little craft before the wind. Where the wind blew he must go and with him his cargo, the fruit at his feet and the forms tied to the grating.

Once with a dangerous and desperate effort he tried to untie them, but his weight thrown to port nearly capsized him. Then, giving the matter up and steeling his heart, he steered before a wind that had now shifted, blowing from the north.

At sunset it was blowing dead from the north and all night long it blew till the dawn rose and there before Rantan, breaking the skyline, palm tops showed and the foam of a tiny atoll singing to the sunrise.

The break was towards the north and the wind brought him through it into the little lagoon, not a mile broad, and on to the beach.

Springing on to the sand and looking wildly around him he saw nothing—only the trees, not a sign of life, only the trees in their beauty, the lagoon in its loveliness, the sky in its purity. Blue and green and the white of coral sand, all in the fresh light of the forenoon Paradise.

Having looked around him, listened and swept the sea with a last glance, he turned to the trees, cast himself in their shadow and leaving the canoe to drift away or stick, fell into a sleep profound as the sleep of the just.

He was saved—for the moment. Freed from Karolin, he had not done with Karolin yet. He had sailed for twenty hours before a five-knot breeze. Karolin was just that distance away below the horizon to the nor'-nor'-west.

BOOK III

I

Le Moan Will Know

The dawn that showed Rantan the tiny atoll awakened Aioma who had fallen asleep thinking of the schooner.

Dick had promised that today they would board her and the canoe-builder in him craved to get to work, and the boy—the boy wanted to sail her, to feel the wind settling in the great spaces of her canvas, to feel her heeling to it like a tilted world, to feel her answering the helm; the canoe-builder wanted to explore her above and below, examine the fastenings of her timbers; her masts and rigging.

Aioma was very old. He might have been a hundred. No man could tell, for Karolin the clockless kept no account of years. He was too old for fighting, having lost the quickness without which a spear- or club-man is of no account as a fighter; but he was not too old for fun.

Whip-ray fishing was fun to Aioma—a sport that, next to conger killing, is the nearest approach to fighting with devils; so also was shaping heavy logs to the form of his dream, for Aioma dreamt his canoes before he shaped them, the breaking of Rantan's joints and the staking him on the reef for sharks to devour would also have been fun had not the women claimed the victim to torture him as they pleased.

Aioma, in fact, was as young as he ever had been and as potent in all fields except those of war and love. He came to the water's edge and stood looking at the schooner. He had dreamt that, walking on the sands of the beach with Taori they had looked for the schooner and found her gone. But she was there right enough, her spars showing against the blaze in the east.

The gulls knew that she was deserted, they flew above her in the golden morning and lighted on her rails and spars whilst the ripple of the tide past her anchor chain showed the living brilliancy of light on moving water.

The canoes and dinghy being destroyed they would have to get off to her in the boat.

For a moment the old man stood looking at the bones of the broken canoes and the planks of the poor old dinghy; the fishing fleet of Karolin had gone just as the fighting fleet had gone, yet the gods had made compensation, for there lay the schooner, a thing more potent than all the fleets of Karolin combined, and there lay her boat, a fine four-oared double-ender, carvel built, white painted, a joy to the eye.

Yesterday at odd times he had examined her outside and in; this morning as his eyes swept over her again, new thoughts came to him and a new vision.

Canoes, what were they beside these things, and why build canoes anymore, why hollow and shape those vast tree-trunks over which they had been labouring for long weeks when here to their hands lay something better than any fleet of canoes? If Taori wished to attack those men on the northern island, why not attack with the schooner, a whole fleet in one piece, so to speak?

As he stood pondering over this new idea, Dick, who had awakened early, came towards him from the trees accompanied by Katafa.

"Taori," said the canoe-builder, "we will go to her (the schooner) you and I; she is ours and I want no other hand to touch her or foot to rest on her till we alone have been with her for a space. Help me." He laid his hand in the gunnels of the boat as he spoke and Dick, as eager as the other, calling to Katafa to help them, went to the opposite side; between them they got her afloat and tumbled in.

Aioma had learned to handle an oar in the dinghy; the heavy ash sweep was nothing to him and as the boat made across the glitter of the lagoon, Katafa, her feet washed by the little waves on the sand, stood watching them.

Dick had not asked her to accompany him. It was as though the schooner had come between them as a rival—a thing, for the moment, more desirable than her.

She was feeling now what she had felt before only more vaguely. She had always distrusted the little ships, those models born of the pocket knife and ingenuity of Kearney, those hints of an outside world, a vague outside world that might some day break into their environment and separate her from Dick.

This distrust had been built up from the cannon shot of the *Portsey* that had smashed her canoe, from the schooner that had come into Palm Tree lagoon with its cargo of Melanesians and it joined with a vague antagonism born of jealousy.

When Dick fell into contemplation of the ship models and especially that of the schooner, he seemed to forget her more completely than even when he was fishing.

Fishing, his mind would be away from her no doubt, but it would still be close; brooding over the little ships and especially the schooner, his mind would be far away. She could tell it by the look in his eyes, by his expression, by his attitude.

And now that this apotheosis of the model schooner was handed to him by the fates as a plaything, the distrust and antagonism in the mind of the girl became acute.

It was almost as though another woman had put a spell upon him alienating him from her. As a matter of fact this was the case, for the schooner was the gift of Le Moan.

As the boat came alongside the *Kermadec*, the gulls left her, drifting off on the wind. Swinging with the tide, her stern was towards the break, the water rippling on the anchor chain which could be followed by the eye through the crystal clear water to where the anchor held in the lagoon floor. The copper sheathing was clearly visible with a few weeds waving from it, fish hung round the stern post and the secret green, the ship-shadow green—the green that is nowhere but in sea water alongside a moored ship—went to Dick's heart as something new, yet old in memory, a last touch to the wonder and enchantment of the hull, the towering masts, the rigging outlined against the diamond-bright blue of the sky.

Tying the boat to the chain plates he scrambled on board followed by the other. Then he stood and looked about him.

His feet had not rested on the deck of a ship since that time when as a tiny child he stood on the deck of the *Rarotonga*, Kearney about to hand him into the shore boat, Lestrange waiting to receive him. So many years ago that time had taken away everything from memory, everything but a vague something that was partly a perfume: the smell of a ship in tropical waters, tar, wood, cordage, all intensified by the tropical sun and mixed with sea scents in one unforgettable bouquet.

He swept the deck with his eyes and then looked aloft. The strange thing was that not only did he know all the important parts of the standing and running rigging, but he knew each part by its name, and by its English name; the only remnants of the language of his childhood were here, attached to the down-hauls, the topping lifts, the halyards, the blocks, taught by Kearney and held tightly to his mind by the model; and Aioma, the old child, voracious in sea matters as the child that once was Dick, knew them too, nearly all, taught to him on the model by Dick.

Master and pupil stood for a moment in silence, looking here, looking there, absorbed, taking possession of her with their minds. Then the pupil suddenly clapping his hands began to run about swinging on to ropes, poking his head here and there, now into the galley, now down the foc'sle hatch.

"It is even as it was in my dream," cried he, "but greater and more beautiful, and she is ours, Taori, and we will take her beyond the reef—*e manta Tia kau*—and we will fill her sails with the wind; she will eat the wind, there will be no wind left for canoes in all the islands." As he chattered and ran about, every now and then his face would turn to port as though he were looking for something. It was the obsession of the outrigger. You will remember that even in his dream when *half an inch high* he had helped to work the model across the rock pool, the dream ship had developed an outrigger; it was so now. The outrigger had so fixed itself in his mind, owing to ancestral and personal experience, as part of the make-up of a sailing craft that Aioma could not escape from the idea of it.

There was something wanting. Reason told him that there was nothing wanting, that the schooner had beam and depth enough to stand up to the wind and sea without capsizing—all the same every now and then, when facing the bow, he was conscious that on his left-hand side there was something wanting, something the absence of which as a stabilizer made him feel insecure.

Dick, having glanced at the compass in the binnacle, of which he could make nothing, turned his attention to the wheel. He had never seen a wheel of any sort before and he had no idea of the use of this strange contrivance. Kearney's ships were all rigged with tillers. Aioma was equally mystified.

"Le Moan will know," said he, "and the men she brought with her. But look, Taori."

He was standing by the saloon hatch and pointing down. He was brave enough on deck, but, like Le Moan, the interior of the schooner daunted him. He had never gone down stairs in his life, nor seen a step, neither had Dick.

The peep down the stairway, the mat below, the vague light through the saloon doorway fascinated Dick without frightening him, and, leaving the other to keep the deck, he came down cautiously, step by step, pausing now and then to listen.

In the saloon he stood looking about him at the handiwork of a civilization of which he knew nothing. The place was in disorder, nothing

HENRY DE VERE STACPOOLE

had been put straight since the fight that still existed in evidence. Bunk-bedding was tossed about, a water bottle lay smashed on the floor by the clothes that once had belonged to Rantan and Carlin. He noticed the telltale compass and the attachments of the swinging lamp, that had been brought on deck, the chairs, the door of the after cabin, the glass of the skylight and portholes, the table on which Rantan had held down Le Moan, the rifles in the rack and the two rifles used by the beachcomber and his companion standing in a corner cleaned and waiting for the deadly work which Le Moan had frustrated.

The smell of the place came to him. The vague odour of sandalwood from the cargo piercing bulkheads and planking, the smell of stale tobacco smoke, fusty bunk-bedding and the trade schooner smell that hinted of cockroaches and coconut oil gone rancid. It seemed part of the place and the place after the first few moments began to repel him.

What came to him through the sense of smell and sight was in fact a waft from the closed spaces of the cities of which he knew nothing, from the men who labour and construct and live and trade crowded like ants under roofs, shut out from the sun and stars and winds of God.

He drew slowly back as though the environment were clinging to him and holding him—but in his hand there was a rifle. Close to him, in the corner by the door, he had seized hold of it. His piercing sight had taken in the shape of the thing used by Rantan in the boat, the thing that spoke so loud and killed at such a distance, and now, seeing the death-dealer so close to his hand, he could not resist it.

He brought it on deck where Aioma was waiting for him and they examined it, but could make nothing of it.

"Let it be," said the canoe-builder, resting it against the coaming of the skylight. "Le Moan will know, or some of those men she has brought with her."

He looked round. Something was troubling his mind. Knowing nothing of the use of the steering wheel he was looking for the tiller.

Dick looked about also. On boarding the schooner he had noticed the absence of a tiller, the most striking object on the deck of the model, but other things had so seized him that he put the question by for the moment.

"No matter," said Aioma, "I know not how we will steer (*accoumi*) when the sails are given to the wind, but Le Moan, she will know."

II

THE THREE GREAT WAVES

The schooner had two boats, the four-oar and a smaller one black painted, battered by rough usage, but still serviceable. Later that day Aioma brought both boats on to the beach for an overhaul.

The remains of Sru and his companions had been dragged by the women to the outer coral and cast at low-tide mark for the sea to dispose of them. Nothing spoke of the tragedy but the remains of the canoes, the planking of the broken dinghy and the ship swinging idly at her moorings.

It was late afternoon and the crew, released from their wives for a moment, sat round whilst Aioma worked. Le Moan sat close to him but apart from the others, amongst whom was Kanoa.

The eyes of Kanoa might wander here or there, towards the canoe-builder, towards the lagoon, towards the schooner, but they always returned to Le Moan, who sat unconscious of his gaze listening to the talk of the old man and the answering words of Poni, whose dialect was the closest to that of Karolin.

Aioma had taken Le Moan off to the schooner that afternoon when he went to fetch the second boat.

It was not really the boat he wanted. His object was to get the girl on board alone with himself so that she might teach him the secret of the tiller and other things so that he might teach Taori. He was not jealous of Taori on land, he had supported him in every way as ruler, but in sea matters and in the mysteries of construction it was just a little hard that he, Aioma, should be less in knowledge than Taori or be condemned to learn with him from the mouth of a girl.

So, not stealing a march on Taori, but at least not awakening him, as the whole village slept in the heat of early afternoon, Aioma had pushed off with the girl and Kanoa, who, being unmarried, was drowsing close under the shelter of a tree.

Leaving Kanoa to keep the boat they had boarded the schooner alone.

Here the girl had explained the mystery of the wheel, the binnacle, in which dwelt a spirit prisoned there by the white men, the winch for getting up the anchor chain. She told him she alone had been able to steer the schooner and she showed him the compass card whose spear head always pointed in one direction no matter how the ship lay.

She did not know how it told the white men where to go, but she thought it must be friendly to Karolin as it had always pointed away from it. If they had obeyed it, they would not have been killed nor the children of Nanu and Ona, nor would Nanti have been wounded (the boy first shot by Carlin and whom Taori had carried off on his back amongst the trees).

"What of that," said Aioma, "children are children, and Nanti will take no hurt. He is already running about and the hole in his thigh will fill up—What of all that, beside the *ayat?*" Yet still his respect for the thing in the binnacle increased, and he followed with his eyes the pointing of the spear head. Why, it was pointing in the direction in which Marua (Palm Tree) lay! Marua, the island of the bad men, who some day—some day would raid Karolin, according to Taori.

He put this matter by in his mind to mature, and then he turned to the last unexplained mystery, the rifle leaning against the saloon skylight just as Dick had left it. She could explain this, too. She had seen Peterson using a rifle for shooting at bottles and her keen eyes had followed everything from the taking of the cartridge from the box to its insertion in the breech, to the act of firing and extraction.

She went to the galley where Carlin had placed the spare ammunition to be handy, and returned with a half full box of cartridges, and, obeying direction, Aioma did everything that Peterson had done. The recoil bruised his shoulder and the noise nearly deafened him, but he was unhurt, neither was the village alarmed owing to the distance, a few birds rose on the reef and that was all. But it was great. The noise delighted him and the smell of the powder. Then leaving the rifle on deck they returned to the beach towing the second boat.

He was talking now as he worked, telling Poni and the others that life on Karolin was not going to be all beer and skittles for them, that as they had joined the tribe and taken wives they would have to work; to work in the paraka patches and in the fishing and to help man the schooner. "For," said Aioma, "there are things to be done beyond the reef, away over there," said he straightening himself for a moment and wiping his brow and pointing north, "where lies Marua, an island of tall trees, and evil men who may yet come in their canoes—no matter. It is not a question for you or for me, but for Taori."

"What you set us to do we will do," said Poni. "We are not beach crabs, but men, Aioma. What say you, Kanoa?"

Kanoa laughed and glanced at Le Moan and then away over the lagoon.

"I will work in the paraka patches and at the fishing," said he, "but the work I would like best would be the work of measuring myself against those evil men you speak of, Aioma—that is the work for a man."

As he spoke the reef trembled and the air shook to a long roll of thunder, an infinite, subdued, volume of sound heart-shaking because its source seemed not in the air above them, but in the earth beneath them and the sea that washed the reef.

The wind had died out at noon, the outer sea was calm and the lagoon, mirror-bright, was making three inch waves on the sand; the tide was at half flood.

Aioma looked about him, the others had risen to their feet and Poni, leaving them, had run on to a higher bit of ground and was looking over the outer sea.

Through the windless air came the outcrying of gulls disturbed and then in the silence following the great sound that had died away, came another silence. The voice of the rollers on the outer beach had almost ceased.

"The sea is going out," cried Poni, "she is leaving us, she is dying—she has ceased to speak!"

As his voice reached them, they saw the water at the break swirling to an outgoing tide: an outgoing tide at half flood!

Led by Aioma they reached the higher ground, stood and gazed at the sea. The vast blue sea glittering without a touch of wind showed like a thing astray and disturbed. Its rhythm had ceased, swell met counter swell, and the Karaka rock spoke in foam; the wet coral showed the fall of the receding tide, and away to eastward white caps on the flawless blue marked the run of the north-flowing current checked for a moment in its course.

The village, disturbed by the vast rumour from the heart of things and answering to the call of Poni, came crowding out from the trees—the women had caught up their children, the boys and young men had seized spears and bows. They glanced to right and left; a woman cried out; then dead silence fell on them. Every eye was fixed on Aioma.

He was standing on a higher piece of coral, mute, motionless, as if carved from rock, his eyes fixed on the troubled waters. Taori might be their chief, but the wisdom of Aioma they knew of old, and seeing him undisturbed, they remained calm, waiting.

The voice of Poni broke the silence:

"She is coming back."

The flood was returning, the swirl at the break had ceased and a wave broke on the coral of the outer beach; the line of white caps died away, the Karaka rock ceased to spout, moment by moment the sea resumed her lost rhythm as breaker on breaker came in filling the air again with the old accustomed sound.

A great sigh went up from the people. All was over.

Yet Aioma did not move.

Dick, who had followed with the others, stood beside Katafa. He noticed that the schooner was swinging back to her old position, the incoming tide setting her again bow to the break, that the sea had regained its accustomed appearance, and that the lagoon was filling. All was right again.

Yet Aioma did not move. He stood with his eyes fixed to the far north. Then, suddenly, he turned and sprang from the rock.

"To the trees—to the trees!" He was no longer a man, he was a whirlwind, he rushed on the people with arms outspread, and, turning, they broke and ran.

"To the trees—to the trees!"

A hundred voices caught up the cry, the groves echoed it in a flash, the beach and coral stood empty, the people had taken to the trees; some to the near trees, some racing along the reef sought the great trees of the canoe-builders.

It was not climbing, as we know it. These people, like the people of Tahiti, could literally walk up a tree, bodies bent, hands clinging to the trunk and feet clutching at the bark.

Katafa could climb like this; Dick, less expert but a good climber, followed her, making her go first, seizing before he left the ground a child that held on to his neck. The child was laughing.

Fifty feet above the ground they clung and looked.

From east to west across the sea stretched a line of light, lovely and strange and infinite in length, swift moving, changing in brilliancy yet ever brilliant. Ever advancing, whilst now from tree top to tree top came the cry, shrill on the windless air:

"*Amiana—amiana!*—the wave—the wave!"

It met the Karaka rock and a great white ghost of foam rose towards the sun. A few seconds later came the boom of the impact followed by the clanging of the reef gulls rising in clouds and spirals; it passed the rock, re-forming, forward sweeping, bearing straight for the reef; a mound of sea towards which the shore waters rushed out as it checked, curved, paled and burst in thunder on the reef, sweeping houses to ruin and flooding into the lagoon.

The trees held though the foam dashed thirty feet up their trunks. Aioma unterrified, with one thought only, the schooner, could see from his eerie that she was safe. Broken by the reef the great wave had not harmed her. But now and again came the cry caught from tree top to tree top.

"*Amiana—amiana!* The wave—the wave!"

The duplicate, the glittering brother of the first long line of light, was moving as swiftly towards them across the sea. Again the Karaka spouted and the gulls clanged out, again the great green hill of water sucked the shore sea to it, curved, crested and broke to the roar of miles and miles of reef.

The bones of the houses broken by the first great comber could be heard washing amidst the tree roots below and from the canoe-builders' grove came the crash of a great tree, a matamata, less secure a refuge than the slender-stemmed coconuts. It had fallen lagoon-ward and the people on it, unkilled, were climbing along it back to shore when yet again came the cry:

"*Amiana—amiana!* The wave—the wave!"

It was the third great wave, bright like a far glittering bar of crystal, scintillating with speed, sweeping through distance as the others had swept towards the reef and lagoon of Karolin.

But now, after the first outcry, the people in the treetops no longer awaited the coming of the danger in silence.

Their spirit suddenly broke. The sight of this third dazzling apparition was too much. What had they done to the sea that she should do this thing to them? Their houses were gone, the trees were beginning to go; the trees would be destroyed and the reef itself would follow them, for what could withstand the enmity of the sea or the night that sent these vast glittering waves unleashed across her, one following on another—with how many more yet to come!

So as the third great wave drew back in silence for its blow against the land, the voice of Karolin was heard, a lamentable voice against the crying of the gulls; children and women and youths and some of the newcome kanakas joined in the cry, but not Le Moan or Katafa, nor Dick. Not Aioma, who, sure of his beloved schooner, found now time and words to comfort his weaker brethren when the comber crashing in spindrift and thunder left the trees still unbroken and a silence through which his voice could be heard.

He called them names that cannot be repeated, but which heartened them up, then he told them that the worst was over and to look at the sea.

Yes, the worst was over. No fourth brilliant line of light showed like the sword blade of Destruction sweeping over the blue, only a greater heave of the swell lifting the inshore green into breakers, horses of the sea resuming their eternal charge against the long line of the reef.

III

THE SECOND APPARITION

Dick was the first person down, followed by Katafa.

He nearly stepped on the spinous back of a great fish, a fish such as he had never seen before, larger than a full-grown man and tangled amongst the bushes and the trees.

The ruin was pitiable. Gone were the great canoe-houses, their thatch and ridgepoles floating in the lagoon water, gone the houses of the village, and all their humble furniture, mats and bowls and shelves, knives, implements and ornaments.

Gone were the little ships and each single thing that Dick and Katafa had brought from Palm Tree; gone was Nan, grin and post and all.

The house of the Uta Matu which, despite its walls of cane and roof of thatch, was in fact a public building, the canoe-houses which were a navy yard—three great waves had washed away all visible sign of the past of Karolin; but the people did not mourn, they were alive and the trees were saved, and the wreckage in the lagoon could be collected and rebuilt into new houses. There were three hours yet before sunset and led by Aioma the salvage hunting began, knives were recovered from cracks in the coral and mats that had wrapped themselves round tree trunks, canes and ridgepoles from the near water of the lagoon; the rainy season was far off and in that sultry weather being roofless was little discomfort; a week or more would put the houses up again, the only serious loss was in the paraka patches, washed clean out. But there was paraka growing on the southern beach, which the waves had not affected, and there was the huge fish of which the sea had made them a present.

Not one of them asked why this thing had occurred, or only Dick of Aioma and Aioma of his own soul.

"I do not know," said Aioma, "only as I stood there I knew in my mind that the sea had not ceased to speak, then I saw the far waves and called to the people to climb the trees."

Of the little ships, not a trace could be found. They had gone forever to some port beyond recall. Dick, to whom these things had been part of his existence, bound up in his life, left Aioma and sat apart by himself brooding as the dusk rose.

The heat had dried up the moisture that had not drained off into the lagoon and the sleeping mats were spread near to where the house of Uta Matu had once stood, but Dick had no heart for sleep.

Not only were the little ships gone, but everything he and Katafa had brought from Palm Tree. But it was the loss of the ships that hurt.

They were his earliest recollection, they were his toys; they had never ceased to be his toys, he who could kill so well and fight so bravely had never tired of them as playthings, playthings sometimes used in play, sometimes forgotten, but always remembered again. Then they were more than that; who can tell how much more, for who can see into the subliminal mind or tell what dim ghosts hiding in the under mind of Dick were connected with these things—Kearney surely, Lestrange and the men of the *Rarotonga*, perhaps. Palm Tree and his life on that enchanted island, certainly.

It was as though Fate, in taking his toys, had cut a cord attaching him to his past and the last remnant of civilization. How completely the hand of Fate had done its work he was yet to know.

The stars showed through the momentary gauze of dusk, and then blazed out over a world of night.

Le Moan, who had refused a mat, was nowhere to be seen. She had slunk away into the tree shadows, where, sitting with her back to a tree bole, she could, unobserved, see the reef and the figure of Dick seated brooding, Katafa's form on the mat where she had lain down to wait for Dick, the foam lifting in the starlight and the sea stars beyond the foam.

What the cassi flowers had said still lingered in the mind of Le Moan.

In that mind so simple, so subtle, so indefinite, so wildly strong, had grown since the night before an energy, calm, patient, sure of itself: a power so large and certain that the thought of Katafa did not even stir jealousy; a passion that could not reason but yet could say, "He is mine, beside me all things are nothing—I want only time."

Katafa had ruined her imaginary world only to create from the ruins this giant whose heart was determination.

Amidst the trees Kanoa, resting on his elbow, could see Le Moan as she sat, her head just outlined in the starlight.

The mind of Kanoa formed a strange contrast to that of the girl. In his mind there was no surety, no calm. Though he had rescued Le Moan, his heart told him that her heart was far from him, she had no eyes for him and though she did not avoid him, he might have been a tree or a rock, so little did his presence move her—and yet, if only she would look at him once, give him recognition by even the lifting of a finger, all his weakness would be turned to strength, his longing to fire.

Presently as the moon rose high, Le Moan's head sank from sight. She had lain herself down and the lovesick one, turning on his side, closed his eyes.

Dick, rising and straightening himself and stretching his arms, turned to where Katafa was waiting for him; he made a step towards her and then stood, his eyes fixed across the northern sea.

Cutting the sky from east to west, bright in the light of the moon lay a cloud, a long thready cloud.

No, it was not a cloud, it was too low. It was different it swelled and contracted, rose and sank.

He called to Katafa and his voice roused Kanoa, whose voice brought Poni from the mammee apple.

In a minute the village was awake and watching this new prodigy, wondering, doubting, the women calling one to the other till the voice of a man rang out:

"Gulls."

A murmur of relief went up from the women.

Gulls, only gulls. Thousands of gulls flying in line formation—and then the murmur checked and died out.

What was driving the gulls?

A storm coming from the north? No, the sky to the north was stainless and to these people who could smell and feel weather, there was no sign of storm.

"Look!" cried Kanoa.

The formation had altered; sweeping round from the east in a grand curve, the great moonlit line was shortening moment by moment till now it had contracted, showing only the van of the oncomers, who were heading for Karolin through the night sky like a spear towards a target.

The sound of them could now be heard, a steady winnowing sound, the pulse-like beat of ten thousand wings, whilst all along the reef from windward and leeward came the crying of the gulls of Karolin.

The crying of the burgomasters and skuas, the frigate birds and the great southern gannets, the laughing gulls and the Brandt's cormorants, all rising like a challenge to the newcomers from whom came no response other than the steady throbbing of the wings.

The gulls of Karolin knew, knew that of which the human beings were ignorant—knew that away beyond the sea line some great home of the sea fowl had vanished beneath the waves as Kingaman island and Lindsay island have vanished in the past, as many a Pacific island will vanish in the years to come. Knew that this was an army of invasion, a fight for a home and fishing rights. Knew that the waters of Karolin and the breeding places were insufficient for themselves and the strangers, knew that the moment which all nations and all wild herds and flocks must face, had come, and then as though actuated by one single mind, rose in a vast ringshaped cloud and swept away south.

Swept away south beneath the moon whilst the van of the invaders now nearly above the reef swerved and turning due west, was followed by the whole line in what seemed, at first, level flight. Then rising and curving in a grand curve like that of a spiral nebula it broke into voice, a challenge that was answered from the south.

"Look!" cried Aioma.

The Karolin birds were returning, drifting like a curl of smoke. A wind seemed blowing them lazily through the sky, a wind seemed moulding them and the invaders, till, in the form of two great vortex rings, they overhung the lagoon: a moment and then clashing in battle, they broke, reformed, and broke again, snowing dead and wounded gulls beneath the moon. The storm of their cries filled the night from reef to reef—now they would be dark against the moon, now away like blown smoke.

Sometimes the battle would drift towards the southern beach only to return gliding towards the northern. It was truly the battle that drifted, not the birds.

Just as a flock flies like one bird, moving here, heading there, under the dominion of a common mind, so these two great flocks fought—each not as a congregation, but as an individual; till, of a sudden and as if at the sounding of a trumpet, the combat broke, the storm ceased, the clouds parted, one still circling above the reef, the other drifting away southeast beneath the moon.

Southeast to find some more likely home, to die in the waves, to split up into companies seeking shelter in the Paumotuan atolls—no man could say, or whether the birds of Karolin were the victors or the strangers from the north. Wanderers lost forever to sight as their home sunk beneath the waves.

IV

What Has Happened to the Reef?

Three weeks' work had recreated the houses broken by the great waves, and put a top knob to the work of the builders. Nan had been recovered. A boy found him cast up in the sand near the break. A new post for him was cut, and Karolin, no longer godless, was itself again. But Aioma was not happy.

The sea when it had swept the reef had not disturbed the tree trunks felled and partly shaped, or had only altered their position slightly as they lay waiting for the canoe-builders to resume work; but Aioma had lost heart in the business. He had come to the conclusion that the schooner was better than any fleet of canoes, and all his desires were fixed on her.

Yet still something called him to the shaping of the logs, the voice of the Unfinished Job perhaps calling to the true workman, or maybe just the voice of habit—all the same he did not turn to it. He was under the spell of the schooner. Pulled this way and that he was unhappy. It is hard to give up a life's vocation even at the call of something better, and he would sit sometimes squatting on the sands, his face turned now to the object of his passion, and now towards the trees that talked to him of the half-born canoes.

Meanwhile in his mind there lay side by side and growing daily, a great curiosity and a great ambition.

The curiosity had been born of the battle of the gulls.

"What," asked he of himself, "has happened to the reef of Marua (Palm Tree)?" He knew Marua, he had been one of the fighters in the great battle of long years ago when the men of the north of Karolin had pursued the men of the south and slain them on Palm Tree beach. He had seen the reef and instinct told him that the invading gulls of three weeks ago had come from there.

They were seeking a new home. Why? What had happened to the reef, or what had driven them from the reef?

Had the great waves of the same day, those three great waves that he still beheld scintillating in his mind, had they destroyed the reef? But how could that be, since they had not destroyed Karolin reef? The whole thing was a mystery and beside the curiosity that it excited, there lay in his mind the great Ambition, to take the schooner into the open sea and sail her there.

The lagoon, great as it was, was too small for him, besides, it was dangerous to the west with shoals and banks.

No, the outer sea was the place for him and there came the rub—Katafa.

Katafa had a horror of the vessel. She would not go on board it and well he knew that Taori would not go any distance from Karolin without Katafa, and he (Aioma) greatly daring, wished to go a long way, even as far as Marua, to see what had happened to the reef.

There you have the whole tangle and you can see how the curiosity and the ambition had grown together whilst lying side by side in his mind.

There was also a scheme.

Katafa would not object to Taori going out in the schooner a little way, and Taori would not mind leaving Katafa for a little time. And, thought the cunning Aioma, once we are out beyond there I will tell him what is in my mind about the gulls and the reef and he will want to go and see; it is not far and the colour of the current will lead us as it always has led the canoes, and the light of Karolin in the sky (*ayamasla*) will lead us back; besides, I will take with me Le Moan, who can find her way without eyes. Cooking this scheme in his mind he said nothing for some days till one evening, getting Taori and Katafa alone with him, he broached the idea of taking the *ayat* out a little way and to his surprise there was no resistance to it on the part of Katafa.

She had seen Dick's face light up at the suggestion. His trouble on account of the lost toys had affected her as though the loss had been her own, and she would say no word to mar this new pleasure, she would even overcome her hatred of the schooner and go with him, if he asked her.

But he did not ask her, he knew her dislike of the ship and the idea of taking her along never occurred to him.

"Then," said Aioma, "tomorrow I will get all things ready with water and fruit, for it is a saying of Karolin that no canoe should ever pass the reef without its drinking nuts lashed to the gratings—one never knows."

"Aie," said Katafa. Then she checked herself and turned away whilst Dick and the old man finished their talk.

They had several names for the sea in Karolin, names to suit its moods in storm and calm; one of these names spoke volumes of past history, history of sufferings endured by canoe men through the ages—The Great Thirst.

The sea to the people of Karolin was not an individual, but almost a multitude; the sea of calm, the sea of storm, the sea that canoe men encountered when blown off shore with the last drinking nut gone—The Great Thirst.

Katafa had known of it all her life. Once she had nearly sailed into it, and the words of Aioma about the water for the *Kermadec* recalled it to her. She shivered, and as the others talked, she scarcely heard their voices, contemplating this new terror which had arisen above her horizon.

But she said nothing, neither that night nor the next day when the casks were being brought on shore to be filled, when the nuts and pandanus fruit were being brought down to the boat by the women, many of them wives of Poni and the others of the crew.

Aioma had told Poni about the coming expedition and the men of the schooner were not only willing to take their places on board again, but eager. Maybe they were tired for a moment of their wives, or just craving for something new—however that may be, they went aboard that night to make preparations for a start on the morrow, leaving their wives on the beach to look after themselves—all but Kanoa.

Kanoa did not go on board. He had had enough experience of that schooner, he did not want to set foot on her again; besides, he wanted to be left behind for his courage was growing and with it the determination to have it out with Le Moan.

So when the others were putting off, Kanoa was not with them. He had gone off along the beach towards the great trees, determining to hide till the schooner was beyond the reef. She was due to go out at dawn or a little later with the ebb tide and he would hide and watching till her topmasts were visible beyond the coral he would come back to the village to find Le Moan.

He would pretend that he had gone fishing on the reef and so had lost the schooner. As he sat down by the great logs of the canoe-builders and watched the stars looking out above the foam, he saw himself returning to the village, the sun in his face, the hateful vessel gone and Le Moan waiting for him.

Kanoa thought in pictures. Pictures suggested to him pictures. He did not know, neither did he picture the fact that Aioma, having decided to take Le Moan with him as a sort of navigating instrument, the girl was at that moment on board of the schooner, asleep, waiting for the dawn, dreaming, if she dreamed at all, of Taori.

V

Mainsail Haul

The dawn rose up on the shoulder of a southeast wind, warm, steady, and breezing the gold of the lagoon water.

Gulls flew about the schooner on board of which Dick and Aioma had slept so as to be ready for an early start.

Now could be heard Aioma's voice calling up the hands from the foc'sle and now Katafa, watching from the shore, could hear the sound of the winch heaving the anchor chain short.

Poni, who had been chief man under Sru, knew all the moves in the game. He watched the mainsail set and the fore, the gaskets taken off the jib; talking to Aioma and explaining things, he waited till the canvas was set and then gave the order for the anchor to be got in.

Le Moan watched as Poni, taking the wheel, let the mainsail fill to the wind that was coming nearly dead from the south, whilst the schooner, moving slowly against the trickle of the ebb, crept up on the village and then turning south in a great curve made for the break on the port tack.

Le Moan could see Katafa far away on the shore backed by the trees of the village, a tiny figure that grew less and less and less as the Gates of Morning widened before them and the thunder of the billows loudened.

The sun had lifted above the sea line and the swell and the wind whipped the spray across the coral of the southern pier whilst Aioma, hypnotized, half terrified, yet showing nothing of it all stood, his dream realized at last.

Oh, but the heart clutch when she heeled to starboard and he recognized that there was no outrigger to port—for the outrigger is always fastened to the port side of canoes—no outrigger to port for the crew to crawl out on and stabilize her by their weight, and when she heeled to port the terror came lest the outrigger should be run too deep under.

There was no outrigger, he knew it—but, just as in the dream ship, he could not get rid of the obsession of it.

Moreover, now that the canvas was raised, now that the wind was bravely filling it, the enormousness of the size of those great sails would have set his teeth chattering had he not clenched his jaws.

HENRY DE VERE STACPOOLE

To take a ship out of Karolin lagoon with the ebb running strong and a south wind, required a cool head and a steady nerve on the part of the steersman. The great lagoon emptying like a bath met the northerly current, the outflowing waters setting up a cross sea. There was also a point where steerage way was lost and it all depended how the ship was set for the opening as to whether she would broach to and be dashed against the coral.

But Poni was used to lagoon waters and the schooner safe in his hands came dead for the centre of the opening; then the ebb took her, like an arrow she came past the piers of coral, met the wash of the cross sea, shook herself and then to the thunder of thrashing, cleared the land and headed north.

"She will eat the wind," Aioma had once said, "there will be no more wind left for canoes in all the islands"; and now as Poni shifted the helm and the main boom stuttered and then lashed out to port, she was eating the wind indeed, the wind that was coming now almost dead aft. The smashing of the seas against her bows had ceased: with a following swell and a following breeze, silence took them—silence broken only by the creak of timber, block and cordage.

Le Moan looked back again. Almost behind them to the sou'-sou'west Karolin lay with the morning splendour on its vast outer beach whose song came faint across the blue sea, on the tall palms bending to the wind, on its gulls forever fishing.

Her eyes trained to great distances could pick out the thicker tree clumps where the houses lay and near the trees on a higher point of coral something that was not coral; the form of a girl, a mote in the sea dazzle now perceived, now gone.

Le Moan watched till the reef line was swallowed by the shimmer from which the trees rose as if footed in the sea. She had stirred no hand in the whole of this business: her coming on board had been at the direction of Aioma, the fate that threw her and Taori together even for a few hours whilst separating him from Katafa was a thing working beyond and outside her, and yet it came to her that all this was part of the message of the cassi flowers, something that had to be because of her love for Taori, something brought into existence by the power of her passion—something that united her forever with Taori.

The mind of Le Moan had no littleness, it was wanting in many things but feeble in nothing; it was merciless but not cruel, and when the sun of Taori shone on it, it showed heights and depths that had only come into being through the shining of that sun. For the sake of Taori she had sacrificed herself to Peterson, for the sake of Taori she had destroyed Carlin, for the sake of Taori she would sacrifice herself again, she who knew not even the meaning of the word "unselfish" or the meaning of the word "pity."

She could have killed Katafa easily, and in some secret manner—but that would not have brought her Taori's love, and to kill the body of Katafa, of what use would that be whilst the image of Katafa endured in Taori's mind.

Katafa was a midge whose buzzing disturbed her dream, it was passing, it would pass.

She turned to where Aioma, who had recovered his assurance and stability of mind, had suddenly flung his arms round Dick, embracing him.

There was something of the schoolgirl in this old gentleman's moments of excitement and expansion, something distinctly feminine in his times of uplift. No longer fearing capsize, free now of the obsession of the outrigger and glorying in the extraordinary and new sensations crowding on him, he remembered the gulls, the reef of Marua and his scheme.

"Taori," cried Aioma, "the canoes I have built, nay the biggest of them, are to this as the chickens of the great gull to their mother. Let the wind follow us till the going down of the sun and we will see Marua."

Dick, for the first time, looked back and saw the far treetops of Karolin. They seemed a vast distance away.

He thought for the first time of Katafa. She had said no word asking him to limit the cruise. Aioma had only suggested taking the ship beyond the reef and the provision of water and fruit had only been taken as a precaution against the dangers of the sea. She had dreaded the business but had spoken no word, fearing to spoil his pleasure, and sure that he would risk nothing for the love of her. But she had reckoned without his youth and the daring which God had implanted in the heart of man; she had reckoned without the extraordinary fascination the schooner exercised upon him and of which she knew next to nothing. She had reckoned without Aioma.

A thread tying his heart to the distant shore twitched as though at the pull of Katafa.

"But Marua is far," said he.

Aioma laughed. "The canoes have often gone there," he replied, "and what are they to this? Besides, Taori, it is no idle journey I wish to make, for it is in my mind that it was from the reef of Marua those gulls came that fought the gulls of Karolin, they were seeking a new home. Why?"

"The gulls only know," replied Dick, "and then there are the bad men whom some day I mean to slay, but not now, for we have not enough men, not a spear with us."

"We have the speak sticks of the papalagi," said Aioma, "and I can use them. Le Moan taught me, but the bad men are out of sight; in this business we need not draw nearer to Marua than we are now from Karolin, or only a little. It is the reef I wish to see and what may walk on it, for gulls do not leave their home just because the wind blows hard or the sea rises high. They have been driven, Taori, and what has driven them—greater gulls, or some new form of man—who knows? But I wish to see."

Dick pondered on this. He had only intended to sail the schooner a short way, to feel her moving on the outer sea, to handle her; with the eating had come the appetite, with the handling of power the desire to use it. He had no fear about getting back, Karolin lagoon light would lead them just as it had led him and Katafa, and his mind was stirred by what Aioma had said about the gulls.

What had happened to drive them away from their home? He had never thought of the matter before in this light, thinking of it now he saw the truth in the words of the other, and having a greater mind than the mind of the canoe-builder, he linked the great waves with the business more definitely than the latter had done.

"Aioma," said he, "the great waves that broke our houses drove the gulls."

"But the waves," said Aioma, "came before the gulls."

"But the gulls may have rested on the water and come after," said Dick, "the waves may have broken the reef as it broke our houses."

"But the reef of Karolin was not broken," said Aioma.

"The waves may have been greater at Marua," replied Dick, "and have grown smaller with the coming."

"I had thought of the waves," said Aioma; "well, we will see; if the reef of Marua is broken, it is broken; if greater gulls are there, we will see them."

Dick looked back once again. The treetops of Karolin so far off now showed only like pins' heads, but the lagoon glow in the sky was definite; ahead could be seen the north-flowing current. Like the *Kuro Shiwo* of Japan, the *Haya e amata* current to the east of Karolin showed a blue deeper than the blue of the surrounding sea; but the *Kuro Shiwo* is vast, many miles in breadth, sweeping across the Pacific from Japan, it comes down the coasts of the Americas—a world within a world, a sea within a sea. The *Haya e Amata* is small, so narrow that its confines can be seen by the practised eyes of the canoe men, and from the deck of the schooner its marking was clearly visible to the eye that knew how to find it; a sharp yet subtle change of colour where the true sea met its river.

Dick could see it as plain as a road. With it for leader and the lagoon light of Karolin for beacon, they could not lose their way. Then there was Le Moan, the pathfinder who could bring them back even though the lagoon light vanished from the sky.

The weather was assured.

Le Moan had taken the wheel from Poni, who wanted to go forward. She, who had brought the schooner to Karolin was, after Aioma and Dick, the chief person on board; in a way she was above them, for neither Dick nor Aioma had yet learned to handle the wheel.

Forward, by the galley, stood the rest of the crew and Dick's eyes having ranged over them, turned to Aioma.

"Yes," said he, "we will go and see." He turned to the after rail. The treetops had vanished, the land gulls were gone, but Karolin still spoke from the great light in the sky that like a faithful soul remained, above all things, beautiful, assured.

VI

Voices of the Sea and Sky

Kanoa, dreading another voyage in the schooner and hating to be parted from Le Moan, hid himself amongst the trees of the canoe-builders.

He was nothing to Le Moan. Though he had saved her from Rantan, he was less to her than the ground she trod on, the sea that washed the reef, the gulls that flew in the air; for these she at least felt, gazed at, followed with her eyes.

When she looked at Kanoa, her gaze passed through him as though he were clear as a rock pool. Not only did she not care for him but she did not know that he cared for her.

Worse than that, she cared for the sun-like Taori. This knowledge had come to Kanoa only the other day.

Sitting beneath a tree, Reason had stood before him and said, "Le Moan does not see you, neither does she see Poni nor Aioma, nor any of the others—Le Moan only sees Taori, her face turns to him always."

As he lay now by the half-shaped logs waiting for the daylight that would take away the schooner, Reason sat with him telling him the same story, the sea helping in the tale and the night wind in the branches above.

It was night with Kanoa, black night, pierced by only one star—the fact that Taori was going away, if even for only a little time. The perfume of the cassi flowers came to him, and now, with the perfume, a far-away voice calling his name.

It was the voice of Poni. The men were going on board the schooner and Poni was collecting the crew.

Again and again came the call, and then the voice ceased and the night resumed its silence, broken only by the wash of the reef and the wind in the trees.

"They will think I have gone fishing," said Kanoa to himself, "or that I have gone on a journey along the reef, or perhaps, that the sea has taken me, but I will not go with them. I will not leave this place that is warm with her footsteps, and on all of which her eyes have rested; the place, moreover, where she is."

He closed his eyes and presently, being young and full of health, he fell asleep.

Dawn roused him.

He could see the light on the early morning sea. The sea grew luminous and the gulls were talking on the wind, the stars were gone, and the ghost of Distance stood in the northern sky blue and gauzy above the travelling sea that now showed the first sun rays level on the swell.

Then Kanoa rose up and came towards the village beyond whose trees the day was burning.

A woman met him and asked where he had been.

"I have been fishing," said Kanoa, "and fell asleep."

He came through the trees till the beach tending towards the break lay before him and the lagoon. The schooner under all plane sail was moving up towards the village and turning in a great curve, but so far out that he could not distinguish the people on deck. He watched her as she came up into the wind and lay over on the port tack. He watched her as she steered, now, close-hauled and straight, for the Gates of Morning, and then he saw her meet the outer sea.

She was gone. Gone for a little time at least; gone and he was left behind, free in the place Le Moan had warmed with her feet, on every part of which her eyes had gazed, and where, moreover, she was living and breathing.

The women had parted with their new husbands the night before. There was no crowd to watch the vessel go out, only Katafa, a few boys and a couple of women who were dragging in a short net which they had put out during the night, using the smaller of the schooner's boats which Aioma had left behind. The women stood for a moment with their eyes sheltered against the sun, then they returned to their work whilst Katafa, leaving the beach, came on to the high coral and to the very point of rock where Aioma, standing, had seen the approach of the giant waves.

She had scarcely slept during the night. Taori was going away from her, nor far or for anytime, but he was going beyond the reef. To the atoll dweller the reef is the boundary of the world—all beyond is undecided and vague and fraught with danger; the comparative peace of the lagoon waters gives the outer sea an appearance of menace which becomes fixed in the mind of the islander and even a short trip away from the harbour of refuge is a thing to be undertaken with precaution.

HENRY DE VERE STACPOOLE

But she had said nothing that might disturb Dick's mind on her account or spoil his pleasure or mar his manhood. Even had the business been visibly dangerous and had Dick chosen to face it, she would not have held out a hand to prevent him. This was a man's business with which womenfolk had nothing to do. So she ate her heart out all the night and stood waving to him as the boat pushed off and watched the *Kermadec* leave the lagoon just as she was watching it now out on the sea, sails bellying to the wind and bow pointing north.

She watched it grow smaller, more gull-like and more forlorn in the vast wastes of water and beneath the vast blue sky. On its deck Le Moan was watching Karolin and its sinking reef just as on the reef Katafa was watching the ship and its disappearing hull, dreaming of wreck, of disaster, of thirst for her beloved one, dreaming nothing of Le Moan.

She watched whilst the morning passed, and the schooner still held her course. "She will soon turn and come back," said Katafa, as the distance widened and the sails grew less, and as the hull sank from sight she strained her eyes thinking that she saw the sails broaden as the ship, tired from going so great a distance and remembering, turned to come back to Katafa.

But the mark on the sky did not broaden. Vaguely triangular and like a fly's wing it stood undecided in the sea dazzle, it seemed to wabble and change in shape and change back again, but it did not increase, and one moment it would be gone and the next it would say "Here I am again, but see how much smaller I have grown!" Then it vanished, vanished for a long time, only to reappear by some trick and again to vanish and not to return.

The sea had taken the schooner and its masts and spars, its sails, its boat; everything that was mirrored only last evening in the lagoon the sea had taken and dissolved and made nothing of. The sea had taken Poni and Timau and Tahuku the strange kanakas; the sea had taken Aioma, and—the sea had taken Taori.

Oh, the grief! The pain that like a knife cut her heart as she gazed on the sea, on the far horizon line above which the speechless sky stood crystal pale sweeping up to azure. He had gone only a little way, soon to return, storms would not come nor would the wind change, nor would it matter if it did change.

Nothing could keep him from coming back. He had food with him in plenty, water in abundance, he had Poni and Timau and Tahuku and

Nanta and Tirai; he had Aioma the wise and he had Le Moan—Le Moan the pathfinder.

Nothing could keep him from coming back and yet the heart of Katafa failed her before that speechless sky and that deserted sea whose meeting lips had closed like the lips of silence upon her lover. Her happiness, so great, perhaps too great, had been cut apart from her for the moment; it stood aside from her never to join her again till Taori came back from what the gods might be doing to him beyond that deserted sea, beneath that speechless sky.

The waters that from all those desert distances drew the voice of indifference and fate that she heard at her feet in the thunder of the breakers, the sky, robbed of speech, yet filled with the ever-lasting complaint of the questing gull.

Someone drew near her. It was Kanoa.

Katafa, who was a friend of all the world, was a friend to Kanoa. She had watched him as he sat apart from the others, noticed his melancholy and spoken to him, asking the reason.

"I am thinking of my home at Vana Vana," had lied Kanoa, "of the tall trees and the village and the reef, of my young days and my people." His young days! He who was still a boy!

"But you will return," said Katafa.

"I do not wish to return," said Kanoa, "I am as one lost at sea, who has become a ghost, and whose foot may no more be set in a canoe and whose hand may no more hold the paddle." Then Katafa knew that he was in love, but with whom she could not tell, nor had she time to watch and find out, being busy.

As he drew near her now, she turned to him, and for a moment almost forgot Dick in her anger.

"Kanoa," said she, "where have you been in hiding? They have gone without you; they called for you and you did not come, and they could not wait. You were wanted to help them in the raising of the sails and the work with the ropes—where have you been in hiding?"

"I have been fishing," said Kanoa.

"And where are the fish?" asked Katafa.

"Oh, Katafa," replied Kanoa, "I hid because I could not leave Le Moan, who is to me as the sun that lights me, who is my heart and the pain in my heart, my eyes and the darkness that blinds them when they see her not. I go to find her now to say to her what I have never said and to die if she turns her face from me."

"And how will you go to find her now?" asked Katafa. "Have you then the wings of the gull and know you not that she has gone with the others?"

"She has gone with the others!"

"She has gone with the others."

Kanoa said nothing. He seemed to wither, his face turned grey, and his eyes sought the distant sea. He, too, had watched the schooner disappear, rejoicing in the fact that she was gone with Taori leaving him (Kanoa) to find his love. And now Le Moan was gone—and with Taori. But he said nothing.

He turned away and lay down with his face hidden in his arms and as Katafa stood watching him, her anger turned to pity.

She came and sat beside him.

"She will return, Kanoa; they will return: he whom I love and she whom you love. They are gone but a little way. It is because they have gone from our sight that we grieve for them. Aioma said they would go but a little way—aie, but my heart is pierced as I talk, Kanoa, my breast is torn; they have gone from our sight and all is darkness. I will see him no more. I will see him no more."

Then, as on the night of the killing of Carlin, the man in Kanoa rose up and cast the boy away; saying not a word about his suspicions of the passion of Le Moan for Taori, he turned to comfort the wildly weeping Katafa.

"They will return," said he, "Aioma is with them and they can come to no harm—they will return before the sun has found the sea or maybe when he rises from it we will see them sailing towards Karolin. Peace, Katafa, we will watch for them, you and I. Go now and sleep and I will wait and watch, and if I see them I will come running to you, and when I sleep you can wait and watch and so with our eyes we will draw them back to us."

Katafa, whose tears had ceased, heaved a deep sigh. She rose and stood, her eyes fixed on the coral at her feet. Weary from want of sleep, she listened to the words of Kanoa as a child might listen, then, without looking once towards the sea, she passed away towards the trees.

Kanoa stood, his gaze fixed on the sea line, and from then through the hours and the days the eyes of the lovers watched and waited for the return of those who had gone "but a little way."

VII

Islands at War—the Open Sea

S omething beside curiosity and the spirit of adventure had made
Dick decide to push on towards Marua (Palm Tree).

The truth is Marua was calling to him. He wished to see it again if
only for a moment. The hilltop and the groves and the coloured birds
sent their voices across the sea to Karolin just as Karolin had sent its
appeal across the sea to Katafa when Katafa had lived at Palm Tree.

As a matter of fact those two islands were forever at war in the battle
ground of the human mind. In the old days natives of Karolin had gone
to live on Marua, and Karolin had pursued them and brought them
back, filling their minds with regret and longing and pictures of the
great sea spaces and free sea beaches of Karolin. In the same way natives
of Marua had gone to live on Karolin and Marua had pursued them
and brought them back, filling their minds with regret for the trees, the
hilltop and the blue ring of the lagoon.

Between Dick and Katafa there was only one faint suspicion of a
dividing line, something that might increase with the years and make
unhappiness the difference between Marua and Karolin: the pull of the
two environments so vastly different, the call of the high island and the
call of the atoll, of the land of Dick's youth and the land of the youth
of Katafa.

It is extraordinary how the soul of man can be pulled this way and
that way by things and forms that seem inanimate and yet can talk—
aye, and express themselves in the most beautiful poetry, strike in their
own defence through the arms of men, follow without moving though
the pursued be half a world away, and inspire a love as lasting as the love
that a man or woman can inspire.

The love of a range of hills, what battles has it not won, and the view
of a distant cloud, to what lengths may it not raise the soul of man—
heights far above the plain where philosophy crawls, heights beyond
the reach of thought.

With the suggestion of Aioma, the concealed longing in the mind
of Dick began to show itself. He forgot Katafa; he forgot the bad men
who had taken possession of Marua, old days began to speak again and

HENRY DE VERE STACPOOLE

the sound of the reef, so different from the voice of Karolin reef, to be heard.

He watched Le Moan at the wheel, and noticed how her eyes followed the almost imperceptible track far to starboard where the water colours changed. She was steering by the current as well as by the sense of direction that told her that Karolin lay behind. He did not know the speed of the schooner, but he had travelled the road when coming to Karolin with Katafa and he knew that soon, very soon, the hilltop of Marua must show.

He went forward and gazed ahead—nothing. The land gulls had been left behind and in all that sea to the north there was nothing. He came aft to find Poni again at the wheel, and as he came he crossed Le Moan who was going forward; she did not look at him and he scarcely looked at her. Le Moan, for Dick, was the girl who had saved them by killing Carlin and fighting with Rantan till he was overcome; but to him, personally, she was nothing. So cunningly had she hidden her heart and mind that not by a glance or the least shade of expression had she betrayed her secret to him. Kanoa only suspected—but he was her lover.

Aioma was squatted on the deck near the steersman, eating bananas and flinging the skins over his shoulder and the rail.

"Aioma," said Dick, "there is no sight of Marua yet, but soon we will see it lifted to the sky, with the trees—it calls to my heart. You have seen it?"

"I was one of those who chased Makara and his men to Marua," said Aioma, "we fought with them and slew them on the beach; aie, those were good times when Uta Matu led us and Laminai beat the drum—*taromba*—that is only beaten for victory, and will never be beaten again, since it went away with Laminai and has never returned. Tell me one thing, Taori. When you came to Karolin with Katafa, you made friends with the women and children, and Katafa told them a tale, how the canoes of Laminai had been broken by a storm, and all his men lost, and how the club of Matu was found by you on the reef of Marua and the gods had declared you were to be our chief. I was on the southern beach at that time and did not hear the tale, but the women and children took it without any talk, glad to have a man to lead them.

"Tell me, Taori, was that all the tale? I never asked you before and I know not why I ask you now."

"Aioma," said Dick, "there was more than that. Laminai and his men came through the woods of Marua and there was a great fight between them and me. I slew with my own hands Laminai and another man. Then, taking fright, all his men ran away and they fought with each other in the woods—many were killed, and then came the big wind from the south and the men who were trying to leave Marua were dashed on the reef, not one being left."

Aioma forgot his bananas. Some instinct had told him that there was more in the story of Katafa than revealed by her to the women, but he had not expected this.

So Laminai, the son of Uta Matu, had been slain by Taori, and his men put to flight; the storm had destroyed them before they could put away, but it would not have destroyed them only for Taori.

He looked up at Taori, standing against the line of the rail, his red-gold head against the patient blue of the sky, and to Aioma it seemed that this journey they had embarked on was no trip to view the outer beach of Marua—that they had been deluded by the guardians of Karolin and the ghosts of the Ancient, drawn to sea to meet the vengeance of the dead Uta Matu, of his son, and the men slain by the hand and will of Taori.

That thunder from the heart of the sea, those waves from nowhere, the prodigy of the gulls, all these were portents.

"Taori," said he, "now that you have told me, I would go back. My heart misgives me and if I had known that Laminai fell by your hand I would not have come; I love you as a son, Taori, you fought for the women and children of Karolin against the white men, but you do not know Uta Matu the king, whose son you killed, whose men you put to flight."

"But Uta Matu is dead," said Dick, "he has no power."

"You do not know Uta Matu," said Aioma, "nor the length of his arm, nor the power of his blow. You have not seen his eyes or you would not say those words. Let us return, Taori, before he draws us too far into his grasp."

"When I have seen what I wish to see, I will return," said Dick. He had no fear of dead men, nor of living men either, and for the first time his respect for Aioma was dimmed. "I will return when I have seen what we came to see. I am not afraid."

Aioma rose and straightened himself.

"I have never known fear," said he, "and I do not know it now. It was for you I spoke. Go forward then, but this I tell you, Taori, there are those against us who being viewless we cannot strike, whose nets are spread for us, whose spears are prepared."

"Aioma," said Dick, "no net can hold me such as you speak of. Nets spread by the viewless ones are for the spirit—*Ananda*—not the body. My spirit is with Katafa, safe in her keeping, how then can Uta Matu seize it?"

"Who knows?" said Aioma. "He is artful as he is strong, and Le Juan who is dead with him is more artful still, and, look, we have the child of Le Juan's daughter with us—Le Moan. Aie! had I thought of all this I never would have brought her."

"How can she hurt us?"

"It is not she. It is Le Juan, the wicked one, whose blood is in her."

To Aioma, as I have said before, people were not dead as they are with us, only removed to a distance, and though he might speak of Spirits, he spoke of people removed out of sight, yet still potent.

He did not believe that Uta Matu could use a real net or spear against Dick, but he did believe that the dead king of Karolin and his witch woman could, in some way, stretch through the distance to lay nets and strike with spears. Ghostly spears and nets not meant for the body, but the man.

If you could have pierced deeper into the mind of Aioma you would have found the belief—never formulated in words—that a man's body was just like the shell of a hermit crab, a thing that could be thrown off, crept out of, discarded. Uta Matu when called into the distance had discarded his shell, but the man and his power remained—at a distance.

"I fear neither Le Juan nor Uta Matu," said Dick, and as he spoke the air suddenly vibrated to the clang of a bell.

VIII

We Shall not See Marua Again

I t was the ship's bell.

Tahuku had struck it in idleness, just as a child might, but the unaccustomed sound coming just then seemed to Aioma a response to the words of the other. But he said nothing. Taori had chosen his path and he must pursue it.

At noon the northern horizon still showed clear and unbroken by any sign of land, yet still the wind blew strong and still the schooner sped like a gull before it.

Tahuku, who had been cook and who knew where the stores were kept, prepared a meal; and whilst the crew were eating, Aioma took the place of the lookout in the bow. Nothing—neither land gull nor trace of land. Nothing but the never ending run of the swell bluer from the southern drift that showed still the contrast of the deeper blue.

A road leading nowhere.

The canoe-builder came up to where Dick was standing in the bow.

"Taori," said Aioma, "we have not lost our way, there runs the current and there Karolin still shows us her light, we have come faster than the big canoes of forty paddles and so have we come since morning, yet Marua is not in sight."

It was late afternoon, and Aioma as he spoke skimmed the sea line from west to east of north with eyes wrinkled against the light.

"No cloud hides it," went on the old man like a child explaining a difficulty, "it is full day, yet it is not there—to our sight."

Dick, as perturbed as Aioma, said nothing. He knew quite well that by now Marua should have been high on the horizon. They had been travelling since morning, how swiftly he could not tell, but with great speed, seeing that they had with them the wind and the current; also the sky stain made by Karolin was now very vague, vague as when he had viewed it from Marua.

"Where then is it gone?" went on the old fellow, "or how is it hidden? Has Uta Matu cast a spell upon us or has Marua been washed away?" Then turning as if from a suddenly glimpsed vision: "Taori—we may sail till the days and the nights are left behind us with the sun and the moon and the stars, but Marua we shall not see again."

Dick still said nothing. He refused to believe that Uta Matu had the power to put a spell on them and he refused to believe that Marua had been washed away by those waves that did little more than smash a few houses at Karolin. All the same he was disturbed. Where then was Marua?

Poni, who was standing near them with Le Moan who had heard what Aioma said, suddenly struck in, in his sing-song voice.

"Surely we passed an island when Pete'son commanded this ship and we were running on this course, an island that would be about here, but is not here anymore—and you remember the great waves that came to us at Karolin and the gulls who sought a home? All these things have just come together in my head as it might be three persons meeting and conversing. Well then, Aioma, it is clear to me now that this island you seek is gone beneath the sea. At the time of the gulls and those great waves, I said to Timan, that somewhere an island had gone under just as Somaya which lay not far from Soma went under in the time before I started to sail in the deep-sea ships. One day it was there and the next day it was not, and there were the big waves just like those that came to Karolin. Marua, you called this island; well, Aioma, you may be sure that Marua has gone under the sea."

And now strangely enough Aioma, so far from accepting the support of this statement, turned upon the unfortunate Poni who had dared to bring experience and common-sense with him to the bar.

"Gone under!" The scream of laughter with which Aioma received this suggestion when it had percolated down into the basement of his intelligence made the faces of the others turn as they stood about near the foc'sle head discussing the same subject.

"Gone under!" What did Poni mean by such silly talk, did he not know that it was impossible for an island to sink in the sea? Sink like a drowning man! No, the great waves had knocked Marua to pieces, either that or Uta Matu had veiled it from their sight. . . and so the talk went on and all the time the sun was falling towards the west and Le Moan's palms were itching to feel again the spokes of the wheel and the kick of the rudder; for a plan had come into the mind of Le Moan, a plan put there maybe by Uta Matu, who can tell; or Passion, who can tell? But a perfectly definite plan to take the wheel, steer through the night and put the schooner absolutely and fatally astray: Put her away from Karolin so far and so much to the east that the lagoon light would be no guide and a course to the south no road of return.

The plan had come to her, fallen into her head, only just now; it was indefinite, but cruelly straight like the flight of an arrow, and in one direction—away from Karolin.

Great love is an energy that, born in mind, has little to do with mind. It is a thing by itself, furiously alive, torturing the body it feeds on and the mind that holds it. Hell is the place where lovers live. Even when they escape from it to heaven as in the case of Katafa, it is always waiting to receive them back, as also in her case.

To Le Moan, dumbly suffering, the message of the cassi flowers telling that Taori was hers by virtue of the power of her passion for him, had suddenly lost all significance. He was here now by the power of the wheel of the ship over the rudder. She could take him away, now, to be always with him—take him away forever from Katafa, steer him into the unknown. And yet the knowledge of this physical power and the determination to use it brought her no ease. She would be close to him, but of what avail is it to a person suffering from the tortures of thirst if he is close to water yet may not drink. All the same she would be close to him.

As she watched the sun so near its setting she dwelt on this fact as a bird on the egg it is hatching, and brooding, she listened whilst Aioma urged that they should turn back at once, and Dick countered the suggestion asking for more time. He had it in his mind to hold on till sunset, till night came to cut them off in the quest. Well knowing in his mind that Marua was no more, that the reef and lagoon and hilltop, the tall trees and coloured birds had all vanished like a picture withdrawn, either gone beneath the sea as Poni said or devoured by the waves as Aioma held—well knowing this in his mind, his heart refused to turn from the quest till turned by darkness.

He would never see Palm Tree again. Like grief for a person lost, the grief of this thing came on him now. He knew now how he loved the trees, the lagoon, the reef, and he recalled them as one recalls the features of the dead. He could not turn till darkness dropped the veil and said to him definitely, "Go back."

He was standing with this feeling in his mind when a sound made him turn to where Aioma had suddenly taken his seat on the edge of the saloon skylight with body bent double and head protuding like the head of a tortoise. He seemed choking. He was laughing.

Aioma, like Sru, had a sense of humour, and a joke, if it were really a good joke, took him like the effect of a dose of strychnine. Sure now that Marua had been swallowed by the sea, the catastrophe, having made itself certain and obtained firm footing in his mind, suddenly presented its humorous side. He had remembered the "bad men." They were swallowed with Marua, he could see them in his imagination swimming like rats, screaming, bubbling—drowning—and the humour of the thing skewered him like a spear in the stomach.

BOOK IV

I

E HAYA

The sun touched the sea line, the blazing water leaping to meet him, and then in a west golden and desolate, in a sea whose water had turned to living light, he began to drown.

Dick watched as the golden brow, almost submerged, showed a lingering crescent of fire and then sank, carrying the day with it as Marua had sunk carrying with it his youth and the last visible threads connecting him with civilization.

He turned. Le Moan had taken the wheel.

The sails that had been golden were now ghost white and a topaz star had already pierced the pansy blue where in the west the new moon hung like a little tilted boat.

"To the south," cried Aioma. "*E Haya*—to the south, Le Moan, to Karolin now that we have seen there is nothing to be seen, to the south; to the south, for I am weary of these waters."

Le Moan, dumb and dim in the starlight now flooding the world, spun the wheel; on the rattle of the rudder chain came the thrashing of canvas and the schooner bowing to the swell lay over on the port tack—due east.

Aioma glanced towards the moon but Le Moan reassured him.

"The current is fighting us," said she, "and I would get beyond it. Have patience, Aioma, the way is clear to me."

He turned away satisfied and lay down on deck. Dick who had brought up some blankets from below to serve as a sleeping mat, lay down by him, and the kanakas, all but Poni and Tahuku, went to their bunks in the foc'sle.

Aioma, lying on his face with his forehead on his arms, heard the rattle of the rudder chain and knew that Le Moan was edging now to the south. She would steer all night with the help of Poni, and sure of her and sure of Karolin showing before them at daybreak, he let his mind wander, now to the canoe-building, now to the spearing of great fish, till sleep took him as it had taken Dick.

Le Moan, steering, could see their bodies in the starlight, and beyond them Poni and Tahuku seated close to the galley, their heads together talking and smoking, heedless of everything but the eternal chatter about nothing which they could keep up for hours together, whilst the schooner under the hands of the steersman was heading again due east.

An hour after midnight the wind shifted, blowing from the west of south. Poni came aft to see if Le Moan wanted anything, food, water, a drinking nut—she wanted nothing; as she had steered all that night long ago towards Karolin, she steered now, tireless, wrapt in herself, without effort.

As the dawn showed in the eastern sky she altered the course to full south and handed the wheel to Poni.

She had done her work, *e Haya,* steered they forever now they would never raise Karolin—so far to the west that even the lagoon light would be all but invisible.

The first sun ray brough Aioma to his feet, he saw Poni at the wheel and Le Moan lying near him fast asleep like a creature caught back into darkness now that her work was done. The sunrise to port told him that the ship was heading south, then he came forward and looked.

The southern sea showed no sign and the southern sky no hint of the great lagoon. Not a bird's wing appeared.

He roused Dick, who came forward and they stood whilst the canoe-builder pointed to the south.

"There is nothing," said Aioma—"yet we have come all the night and she is never wrong—not even the light in the sky. Yet by now the trees should have shown."

Dick, gazing into the remote south at the blue and perfect and pitiless sky, unbroken at the sea line, unstained above it, drew in his breath; a cold hand seemed placed on his heart. Where then was Karolin?

"Who knows," said Aioma, "it may show when the sun is higher. Let us wait."

They waited and watched whilst the sun rose in the sky, but the sun revealed nothing that the dawn had not shown—nothing save away to the westward unseen by them and so faint as scarcely to be seen, a pale spot in the higher blue—the light of Karolin.

Aioma came running aft. He shook Le Moan and roused her from her sleep and she came forward and stood in the bow, sheltering her eyes against the light.

"It is not there," said she; "I can see nothing with my eyes nor in my mind—the power has gone from me, Aioma, it has been taken from me in my sleep."

Aioma struck his head with the flat of his hand, then he turned to her as she stood there with the lie on her lips, close to, almost touching Dick, who stood, his hand on the rail, scarcely breathing.

"Gone from you," cried the canoe-builder, "taken in sleep, aie, what is this! We are adrift and astray, gone! And who could take it but Uta Matu. Taori, we are lost, we are in the hands of the viewless ones; their nets have taken us. I told you this, yet you would not put back. Never more shall we see Karolin."

Dick did not move. He saw again the figure of Katafa as she stood on the beach when they were leaving, that loved figure from which he had parted with scarcely a thought, so full was he of the schooner and the dream of sailing her on the outer sea. Katafa who even then was watching for him away beneath that tiny stain on the western sky, grown so faint now as to be almost invisible.

Even last night when sure of return, his heart had longed for her, he had dreamed of her; by a thousand little threads, each living, she had joined herself to his very being, and he would never see her again!

"Never more shall we see Karolin." He turned to the desolate south, to the west, to the east; then, heedless of the others, a savage in his grief, he cast himself on the deck, his face on his arms as if to hide himself from the hateful sun.

II

Aioma Curses the Wind

N ever more shall we see Karolin."

The words of Aioma were repeated by the sky, by the sun, and the sea. Never more would he see Katafa, hear her voice, feel her arms about him. The hard hot deck beneath him, the sun beating on his back, the sounds of the sea on the planking and the groaning of the timbers all were part of his misery, of the awful hunger that fed on his heart.

He loved her as a man loves a woman, as a child loves a mother, as a mother loves a child. He who had killed men and dared death was, in fact, still a child; passionate, loving, ignorant of the terrors that life holds for the heart of man, of the grief that kills and the separation that annihilates. He had never met grief before.

Le Moan watched him as he lay. She knew. He was lying like that because of Katafa, she had lain like that on the coral because of him.

By declaring that vision had returned to her, by seizing the wheel and steering for Karolin, she could have brought him to his feet a well man—only to hand him over to Katafa.

She could not do that.

Her heart, pitiless to the world, was human only towards him; she had braved the unknown and she had braved death to save his life, but to save him from this suffering she could not speak three words.

Aioma watched him absolutely unmoved. If Dick had been wounded by a spear or club, it would have been different, but mental anguish was unknown to the canoe-builder and you cannot sympathize with the unknown.

Then as Dick struggled to his feet and stood with his hand on the rail, dazed and with his face turned again to the south, the old man recommenced his plaint with the insistency of a brute, whilst the wind blew and Poni at the wheel kept the ship on her course south, ever towards the hopeless south.

"No," said Aioma, "never more shall we see Karolin. Uta has us in his net. Never more shall I shape my logs (he had dropped that business before leaving Karolin) or spear the big fish by night whilst the boys hold the torches (*upoli*), and the great eels will go through the water with none to catch them. It is this *ayat* that has brought us where we now are to confusion and a sea without measure, and this wind, which is the breath of Le Juan, and may her breath be accursed. Well, Taori, and so it stands, and what now? Shall we go before the wind or counter it—seek the south *e Haya* where nothing is, or the east *e Hola* where nothing is?"

Dick turned his face to the canoe builder. "I do not know, Aioma, I do not know. It is all darkness." His eyes turned to Le Moan and passed her, falling on Poni at the wheel, and the sea beyond.

Aioma had told him that he was taking Le Moan as a pathfinder, but Dick had troubled little about that, scarcely believing in it. He had trusted to the current and the light of Karolin as a guide. They were gone, but it was the words of Aioma that removed the last vestige of hope.

He trusted Aioma in all sea matters and when Aioma said that they were lost, they were lost indeed. Palm Tree vanished, Karolin gone, nothing but the sea, the trackless hopeless sea and the words of Aioma!

Urged by a blind instinct to get away from the sight of that sea, that sky, that pitiless sun, he left the deck and came down the steps to the saloon where he stood, a strange figure, almost nude, against the commonplace surroundings; the table, the chairs, the bunks with their still disordered bedding, the mirror let into the forward bulkhead, a mirror so old and dim and spotted that it scarcely cast a reflection.

He looked about him for a moment, moved towards the bunk where Carlin had once slept, and, sitting down on the edge of it, leaned forward, his arms resting on his knees, his head bowed; just as his father had sat long, long years ago when Emmeline had vanished into the woods to return bearing a child in her arms—bearing him, Taori.

Just as his father had sat all astray, crushed, helpless and lost, so he sat now, and for the same reason.

Up on deck Poni at the wheel turned to the canoe-builder.

"And what now, Aioma," said Poni, "since Le Moan knows not where to go, where go we?" As he spoke the mainsail trembled, rippled, and flattened again.

The canoe-builder turned aft. The breezed-up blue, beyond a certain point, lay in meadows and a far glitter spoke of a great space where there was no wind.

"The wind is losing its feathers," said Poni with a backward glance in the direction towards which the other was looking.

As he spoke the mainsail trembled again as though a shudder were running up it and the boom shifted to the cordy creak of the topping lifts.

Yes, the wind was losing its feathers, dying, jaded, exhausted; again the mainsail flattened, shivered and filled only to flatten again, the wabble of the bow wash began to die out and the schooner to lose steerage way.

The breath of Le Juan was failing and Aioma who had cursed it saw now the calm spreading towards them, passing them, taking the southern sea.

Poni left the wheel.

There was nothing to steer. A ship is only a ship when she is moving, and the schooner, now a hulk on the lift of the swell, lay with a gentle roll on the glassy water—drawing vague figures upon the sky with her trucks, complaining with the voice of block and cordage whilst the canoe-builder standing with his eyes on the north, felt the calm: felt it with a sixth sense gained from close on a century of weather influence; measured it, and knew that it was great. Great and enduring because of its extent, complete and flawless as a block of crystal placed by the gods on the face of ten thousand square miles of sea.

He remembered how he had cursed the wind, and turning to speak to Le Moan, found her gone.

Le Moan following Dick to the saloon hatch had stood for a moment listening.

Unable to hear anything below, she waited till Aioma's back was turned and then cautiously began to descend the steps of the companion-way; cautiously, just as she had come down those steps that night to attack the white men single-handed and save, at the risk of her life, the life of Taori.

Reaching the door of the saloon, she saw him half seated on the bunk's edge, his elbows on his knees and his face in his hands whilst above him, now on the ceiling, now on the wall, glimmered and glittered and danced the same water shimmer that had danced above the sleeping Carlin. Only now it was a butterfly of gold.

The ripples sent out by the roll of the schooner on the sea surface gave it its tremor, the roll its extent of flight, the sunlight its gold.

It fluttered now, sweeping down as if to light on Dick, and now it was flying on the ceiling above him. It seemed a portent, but of what she could not tell, nor did she heed it after the first glance.

Crossing the floor, she came to him, sat down beside him, and rested her hand on his shoulder.

Dick turned to her. Like the child that he was, he had shuddered and sobbed himself into a state where thought scarcely existed above the sense of despair. He turned to her, the touch of a woman's sympathy relaxing the numbing grip of Disaster, yet not for a moment releasing him. Then casting his arms around her neck, he clung to her for comfort as a child to its mother.

Clasping her arms around his naked body, her lips on his throat, her eyes closed, in Paradise—heedless of life and death and dead to the world, Le Moan held him, flesh to flesh, soul to soul, for one supreme moment her own. That she was nothing to him was naught, that grief not love had thrown him into her arms was naught, she held him.

To Le Moan whose soul was, in a way, and as far as Taori was concerned, greater than her body, marriage and its consummation could have given little more—if as much. She held him.

Above them danced the golden butterfly that no man could catch or brutalize; a thing born of light, of the sea, of chance; gold by day that had been silver by moonlight, elusive as the dreams that had led Carlin to his death and the love that had led Le Moan to destroy him.

Then, little by little, the world broke in upon her, her arms relaxed, and rising, half blind and groping her way, she found the door, the steps, the deck, where Poni stood released from the wheel, and Aioma by the rail.

III

He Has Turned His Face from the Sun

The Ocean is a congregation of rivers, the drift currents and the stream currents; rivers, some constant in their flow, some intermittent and variable; some wide, as in the case of the Brazil current which at its broadest covers four hundred and fifty miles; some narrow as in the case of the Karolin-Marua drift, scarcely twenty miles from east to west. The speed of these rivers varies from five miles a day to fifteen or thirty, as in the case of the Brazil current, or from ten to a hundred and twenty miles a day as in the case of the Gulf Stream.

Sometimes these rivers, lying almost side by side, are flowing in opposite directions, as in the case of the north running Karolin-Marua current and the southerly drift that had now got the schooner in its grasp; and each one of these streams of the sea, from the Arctic to the Antarctic, has its own peculiar people, from the Japanese swordfish of the *Kuro Shiwo* to the Gambier turtles on the Karolin-Marua.

Left without wind the schooner drifted, her sails casting vast reflections on the glassy swell; sometimes, away out, a slight disturbance on the water would show where a sleeping turtle had suddenly submerged, and over-side in the ship's shadow, fucus and jelly-fish floating fathoms deep could be seen drifting with the ship. Nothing else. Neither shark nor albacore nor palu nor gull spoke of life across or beneath that glacial sea.

The sun sank in a west of solid gold and the stars took the night, the sails showing black against the brilliant ceiling.

Dick, who had come on deck before sunset, stood by Aioma at the after rail. He seemed himself again, but he had not eaten that day; a fact that disturbed the canoe-builder, who had turned from dark thoughts and misgivings to a sort of cheery fatalism. Aioma was alive and there was food and water on board for a long time and the wind might blow soon or the drift—he sensed a drift—take them somewhere. He had a feeling also that his curses had closed the mouth of Le Juan; he had eaten well, and his belly was full of ship's food and bananas, so his sturdy nature refused depression.

"Of what use," he was saying, "is a man without food? A man is the paraka he eats and the fish. . . Go and eat, Taori, for without food a man is not a man."

"I will eat tomorrow," said Taori, "I have no heart for eating now."

Away forward crouching in her old place Le Moan listened to the creak of the ship as it moved to the swell and watched the stars that shone on Karolin.

The faithful unbreakable sense born with her as truly as the power of the water-finder is born in him, or the power of the swallow to find its southern nest, told her just where Karolin lay; away on the starboard beam to the north, now dead aft as the schooner turned to some gentle swirl of the current, now a bit to port, now back again to starboard.

She could see the figures of Taori and Aioma in the starlight and she could hear the voices of Poni and the others from the foc'sle, the creak of the timbers and the creak of the main boom as it moved to the rocking of the swell. She too had not eaten that day.

She had done her work and she had received her reward. With his body in her arms and her lips on his neck, she had drunk him as a creature dying of thirst might drink long delicious draughts from a poisoned well; for he had clung to her not in the passion of love, but of misery, and he had let her hold him as a comforter not as a lover, and she knew that till the stars fell dead and the sun ceased to shine that never would he be closer to her than that.

This knowledge had come to her from the very contact with his body, from the clasp of his arms about her neck. He had told her unconsciously and without speech more than he could have ever have told her in words. He was Katafa's.

He was forever out of her reach, sure and certain instinct told her that, yet he was near her and she could see him—they were together.

Only a little before sundown Aioma had said to her, "Le Moan, maybe since the wind has gone the spell of Uta Matu has ceased to work. Shut your eyes, turn, and see if you cannot get a view again of where Karolin lies; is the sight of it still gone from you, Le Moan?"

"It is still gone," she had answered him, "and even if it were with me, of what use, for there is no wind?"

She had told the lie looking him in the face and seeing only Taori.

It was no little jealousy that made her lie; she had no jealousy towards Katafa whom Fate had bound to Taori before she had seen him. He had not chosen Katafa in preference to her; perhaps that was why her heart held no jealousy. All the same to bring him back, to take the wheel and steer him into the arms of Katafa—she could not.

To save his life she could easily have died for him, to give him back to joy and love was impossible.

The night passed and the sun rose on another day of calm, and still the schooner drifted, the variable current setting her back sometimes, sometimes leading her a bit more south. Truly it was a great calm as Aioma had predicted and it fell on Taori, as on the sea, like the hand of death. He scarcely ate at all; he had fallen away from himself, his mind seemed far away, he scarcely spoke.

As men who have never met the microbes of disease fall easily victims and die when other men only fall ill, Taori, who had never before known grief, in the language of Aioma, turned his face from the sun.

On Karolin men had often died like that, of no disease—because of insult, because of a woman, sometimes just for some reason that seemed trivial. It is one of the strangest attributes of the kanaka, this power of departing from the world when life becomes unendurable, too heavy or even just wearisome.

"He has turned his face from the sun," said Aioma to Poni one morning—the fourth morning of the calm—and Le Moan who was nearby heard the words.

It was on that same morning that the breeze came, a light air from the north strengthening to a steady sailing wind, and almost on the breeze came the call of the look-out who had climbed to the cross-trees.

"Land!"

Just a few palm tree tops to the southeast, the trees of a tiny atoll, so small that it cast no lagoon reflection; and Aioma who had climbed to see came down again whilst Poni, who had taken the wheel, put the ship to the southeast taking his position from the sun not far above the eastern skyline.

Presently the far-off treetops could be seen from the deck, but Dick as Poni steered, and after a glance at the distant trees, lost interest.

He had turned his face from the sun.

IV

What Happened to Rantan

When Rantan awoke from sleep it was morning. He had slept the clock round. He awoke hungry and full of vigour, and coming out from amongst the trees he stood for a moment by the edge of the little lagoon above whose sapphire waters the white gulls were flighting against a sky new-born and lovely and filled with distance and light.

The canoe lay where he had left it, high-beached now, for the tide was out. The bodies that had been tied to the gratings were gone, the gulls had done their work, and nothing showed but the coconut sennit bindings hanging brown like rags and moving to the breeze.

Close to the northernmost of the trees lay a little pond from which he had drunk before lying down; the trees stretching from the pool ran in a dense line for a quarter of a mile, pandanus, coconut palm, bread fruit, and a dense growth of mammee apple, shading beach and reef to a spot where the naked reef took charge. The rest of the ring of the atoll showed few trees, just a small clump or two of fifty-foot palms, wand-like and feathery against the blazing blue.

There was food here, enough of a sort, but he had neither knife nor fire nor fishing line. He was naked.

When they had bound him and kept him and flung him in the canoe to take him to the southern beach of Karolin, he had not bothered about the fact that he was naked—it had not troubled him at all till now. Now that sleep had restored him to himself, the fact of his nakedness came to him as a sudden trouble making him forget for the moment everything else, even food.

The trouble was entirely psychical. The climate of the beach was so warm that he did not require clothing as a protection, and there was shade enough to shelter him from the sun if he were too warm. All the same, his nakedness lay on him like a curse. He felt helpless, part of his environment that had clung to him for forty years was gone from him and without it he was all astray; naked as a worm he felt useless as a worm, ready to flinch at anything, without initiative, without power.

Dick had never known the need of clothes, he had never worn them. It was different with Rantan.

The absence of shoes he felt less, though without them he was condemned to keep off the rough coral and keep to the beach sands.

He came along the sands towards the canoe. Had you been watching him and had he been clothed in purple and fine linen you still would have said to yourself "There is something wrong about that man, why does he walk like that?"

When he reached the canoe he looked in at the remains of the fruit all squashed and gone bad from the sun; then, turning to the gratings he began to unfasten the strips of coconut sennit that had tied the bodies of the children.

The birds had pulled the bodies to pieces, not even the little bones were left and the bindings hung lax; his fingers were not trembling now as they had trembled on Karolin when trying to untie the knots; he had plenty of time to work in and bit by bit the fastenings came undone.

Then the gulls, if they had bothered to look, might have seen a strange sight: Rantan trying to make himself a loin cloth.

Why?

He had neither real decency nor shame in his composition, there was no one to see him in his nakedness but the gulls. Why then did he trouble?

Trouble he did and the result was scarcely worth his trouble. Then, and still without eating, he turned to and cleared the rotting pandanus and other fruit out of the canoe—he could not swill her out as he had nothing with which to hold water, but she had brought in a long piece of weed tangled on the outrigger; the sun had dried it, but he wet it again in the lagoon water and used it as a sort of mop.

Having cleaned her and seen that the mast, sail and paddles were all right, he came back to the trees, plucked some pandanus drupes and began to eat.

As he sat down to the food, he made to hitch up his left trousers leg, a habit he had. Before leaving the canoe to come back to the trees he had tried to put his hand in his pocket. In this way and in other ways and incessantly his vanished clothes spoke to him, reminding him that he was naked, worm-naked on the face of the world.

He ate, staring at the lagoon as if hypnotized by its blueness, and as he ate, pictures travelled before his mind's eye, pictures of Karolin lagoon and the two dead women he had left on the southern beach, and then, as a bird hops from one branch to another, his mind left Karolin and lit on the deck of the *Kermadec* and from that on to the sands of Levua in whose woods he had slain Peterson.

All his troubles had started from the killing of Peterson. It was just as though Peterson had been following him, stripping him steadily and bit by bit of everything down to his very clothes: of the schooner, of the pearl lagoon, of his sea chest, of the few dollars he had saved, of his hat, his shoes, his trousers, his shirt, his coat—everything. He tried to put away this idea but failed.

It was now only nine o'clock in the morning of a day that would not end at sunset, of a blue and blazing day that, with night intermissions, would last for months and months—for the rainy season was far off. And he was out of trade tracks.

He stood up, looked about him, and then walking carefully, picked his way on to the rough coral above the outer beach. Here on a smooth spot he stood looking over the sea to the northeast.

Nothing.

Karolin, with fabulous treasure in its blue heart, lay somewhere over there, lost, so far that even the lagoon light did not show.

He turned to the southeast. Somewhere there lay the Paumotus.

Should he push off in the canoe and try to reach them?

Since waking this morning there had fallen upon Rantan a double obsession, the paralysing sense of his nakedness and now the feeling that somehow in some way Peterson was following him—following him wearing the seven-league boots of bad luck. He believed neither in God nor in ghosts, but he believed in luck—and his luck had been frightful and it had dated from the killing of Peterson.

This double obsession cut the ground from under the feet of his energy, so that the idea of escape in the canoe entered his mind only to leave it again. He came back to the trees, lay down in their shadow and now the gulls began to talk to him.

The little island had two voices, the endless sound of the breakers and the unending complaint of the gulls; sometimes it would be just a voice or two, sometimes clamour—always indifference, voices from a world that knew nothing of man.

The dead women he had left lying on Karolin beach were not further beyond the pale of things than he who had slain them, and it came to Rantan as he lay there that he was shut out; no one knew of his fate, he was of no manner of interest to anything that surrounded him; to the wind, to the sunlight, to the trees, to the gulls. If he were to drop dead on the sands, he would become an object of interest to the predatory gulls, but alive he was of interest to nothing.

This was not a passing thought; it was kept alive in his mind by his nakedness. His mind had been stripped of its clothes in the form of living beings and accustomed surroundings, just as his body had been stripped of its clothes in the form of shirt, coat and trousers. The two nakednesses were as two voices perpetually talking together, answering each other, echoing one another.

Then, hypnotized by the murmur of the reef, he drifted off into sleep.

He was on the schooner. She was anchored in Karolin lagoon and the crew were diving for pearls, the deck was strewn with heaps of shells and Carlin was showing him a huge pearl in the palm of his hand. It was the last, they had stripped the lagoon clean, and now it was mainsail haul for 'Frisco, wealth, wine and women. He was down in the cabin, pearls all over the floor and pearls in the bunks, and as the ship rolled, the pearls ran and he chased them about the floor on his hands and knees, and they turned into pebbles as he caught them. Some turned into white mice and ran over Carlin who was lying dead by his bunk, and then Poni shoved his head through the skylight and called down at him: "Caa—caa—caa," and he awoke beneath the trees to the call of a passing gull.

V

What Happened to Rantan (continued)

He sprang to his feet and came running out on to the sands. For a moment he could not tell where he was, then he remembered.

It was past noon and the tide was beginning to ebb. He saw the canoe and he stood, stood for a full minute without moving a single muscle—his mind working furiously, no longer diffident, no longer helpless, as though the dream in restoring his old environment had given him strength, renewed courage and daring.

He must clear out of this place, get to the open sea. The Paumotus were possible, ships were possible, death was possible, but better than this place where nothing was possible, where nothing was but a beach to walk on, blazing sun and jeering gulls.

The ebb was beginning to run, it would take him through the break, he must act at once.

He ran towards the trees and began collecting pandanus drupes and carrying them to the canoe. He climbed like a monkey for drinking nuts, and just as on the Karolin beach he ran, sweating as he came piling the fruit on board; drinking nuts, drinking nuts—he never could have enough of them. Then the last of his frantically collected cargo on board he did what he had also done on the beach of Karolin, flung himself down by the little pool and drank till he nearly burst.

It was all a repetition of that business and only wanted the dead bodies of the women to make the picture complete. Then he came to the canoe.

Here it was the same again. He could not get her off. The dead children no longer weighed down the outrigger, but he had stowed his cargo badly and that did the business; the outrigger was bedded in the sand. He laboured and sweat rearranging the fruit, then at last she began to move; he pushed and drove, the lagoon water took her to amidships—another effort and she was water-borne and he was on board working with a single paddle and getting her farther out.

He was free.

A weight seemed gone from his soul, he no longer felt his nakedness, the power of movement, the escape from the beach and the new hope that lay in the open sea, were like wine to his spirit. It was a move in a new game and daring whispered to him that he would yet beat Peterson.

Working with the paddle from side to side, he got her farther and farther out, and the break lay before him now and beyond the break beckoned the sea.

He had turned sideways to take a last derisive look at the prison house of the trees and beach when—aye, what was that? Water ran over his knees as he knelt to the paddling, water that moved with a slobber and chuckle beneath the nuts.

The canoe was leaking. The sun must have done this business yesterday, craftily, whilst he was asleep. She had been bone dry when he stowed the fruit and now the stuff was awash or nearly so.

The mat sail was brailed ready to be broken out when clear of the lagoon. He looked at it, then his eyes fell again to the interior of the canoe—the water had risen higher still: this was no ordinary leak that immersion would caulk, there was nothing to be done but to return and try to mend it on the beach.

He began to paddle, making frantic efforts to turn the canoe's head and bring her ashore. He was too late, the ebb had her like a leaf and though he turned her head, it was only to make her float broadside to the spate of the tide.

The only chance was to try and hit the beach near the break.

He worked like a giant.

Only a few minutes before his heart had rejoiced at his escape, now, with the prospect of certain death from drowning in the outer sea, the beach seemed to him the most delectable place in the world.

But he could not reach it. The nearer the break the swifter the ebb; the lagoon water had him like a swiftly running river; the canoe twisted and turned to his efforts but he could not alter the line of its travel sufficiently to hit the beach.

Then, flinging the paddle away he rose, held on to the mast, plunged over the side and struck out for the shore.

When he reached it and stood up, the canoe was gone, swept to sea to be submerged and tossed on the swell.

His last possession had been taken from him. Schooner, money, pearls, clothes and lastly the canoe, all were gone; he had nothing in the world—save the loin cloth made from the bindings of the dead children.

But he was not thinking of that. His life had been saved. He had almost touched death and now as he looked on the oiling current, he saw a shark fin shearing along as though the shark that had missed him was blindly hunting for him.

He came back to the trees, hugging the life that had been spared to him and sat down to rest, Death sitting opposite to him—cheated.

This business brought things to a crisis with Rantan; though robbing him of his last possession, it still had given him a sense of winning a move, and truly, though his luck had been dreadful, there had been an undercurrent of good luck. He had escaped from Le Moan that night, he had escaped from Nanu and Ona who had him bound hand and foot, he had escaped from the sea coming to this atoll, and he had escaped from the leaking canoe and the shark. His mind took a turn. He felt that he was meant to live, he was sure that now he would be rescued. A ship would come.

And at this thought that seemed clothed in surety, the man's soul blazed up against Karolin. If she were only a ship with the right sort of people on board, he would find Karolin for them and they would rip the floor out of that lagoon and the hearts out of the kanakas that lived by it.

And the right sort of people would be on that ship and she would come—she would come. He knew it.

What Happened to Rantan (continued)

He fell asleep on the thought and for days and days he hugged it, and everyday a dozen times he would go to the flat space on the coral and look over the sea for the ship.

One morning he saw something dark on the beach near the break; it was the canoe, the tide had taken her out only a little way and the sea had played with her, submerged as she was, returning her to the lagoon where the full flood had beached her. The water had drained out of her with the ebb and there she was and there he found her, pulling her up higher just for something to do. He found the crack that made the leak, it was quite small and he might have plugged it, but there was no paddle and anyway he would not have used her—he was waiting for the ship that was sure to come.

Rantan had, like most sailors, the full use of his hands, and he longed to use them, but he had no tools or anything to work on; near the trees and close to the mammee apple there was a patch of coarse grass and the idea came to him to make something out of it. Once in Chile he had escaped from prison by making a grass rope and the idea came to him now to make another; anything was better than sitting in idleness, and it seemed a lucky thing to do, for not only had he escaped from the Chilean prison by means of the rope, but he had come on a streak of good luck when free. So, gathering grass, he sat down to weave his rope.

The business was a godsend to him.

He limited the work to a few hours a day so as not to cloy himself, and he would look forward to the work hours as men look forward to a smoke.

Whilst he worked at it, he wove his thoughts into the rope, his desires, dreams and ambitions all were woven into it, the killing of Peterson went in, and the memory of the dead women on Karolin beach, his hatred of the kanakas and of the red-headed one who had come and looked at him, Dick.

As a woman weaves into her knitting her household affairs and so on, the busy fingers of Rantan wove into his rope visions of ripping the pearls out of Karolin lagoon, of hunting the kanakas to death, of drinking bars and loose pleasures to be had with the pearl money—truly, if an inanimate thing could be evil, it was evil, for it held Rantan's past. The amount of grass being limited, he sometimes knocked off work for a couple of days; and the days became weeks and the weeks went on and on till one morning, when the grass being nearly finished and the rope almost long enough to hang a man with a six-foot drop, Rantan, coming to his lookout, sighted a ship.

Away towards the north she lay so far that he could only tell she was of fore and aft rig and making either for or away from the atoll. Ten minutes showed her bigger—she was coming for the atoll. She was The Ship.

Then Rantan danced and sang on the smooth bit of coral and shouted to the gulls, and he came down to the sands and ran about on them like a dog in high spirits; he shouted to the canoe and abused her and called her filthy names, then back again to see how the ship was growing and back again to the sands to cut more capers.

She grew.

Returning to his lookout post for the fourth time, she seemed to have suddenly shot up in size as if by magic. Now he could see her clearly, her make and size and the patch on her foresail. He took a breath so deep that his chest stood out above his lean belly like a barrel. God! she was the *Kermadec!* The *Kermadec* or a sister ship, her twin image; the eye of a sailor told him that, the patch on the foresail he knew—he had helped to put it there.

He turned and came running on to the sands.

White men must have come into Karolin lagoon and made friends of the kanakas—the women would have been found dead on the beach, the canoe gone. It was all plain.

They would know that with the wind blowing at that time the canoe would have come in this direction; he was being searched for, either to be clubbed to death by kanakas or hanged by whites.

There lay the canoe on the beach and his footsteps on the sand.

He looked round. There was no mark of a campfire to give him away, nothing but the canoe, the footsteps, the fruit skins and coconut shells he had left lying about, and the rope.

He started to clear up, casting the skins and shells amongst the bushes. Then, diving into the bushes he hid there listening—waiting, sweating, the rope coiled by his side.

VII

The Battle and the Victory

The island grew.

Poni at the wheel, his eyes wrinkled against the sun, steered; Aioma beside him, Le Moan near Aioma and Dick forward near the galley. Dick had taken his seat on the deck in a patch of shadow and now he was leaning on his side supporting himself with his elbow. The sight of this island that was not Karolin had completed the business for Dick.

For four days he had scarcely touched food and for four days Le Moan had watched him falling away from himself. It was like watching a tree wither.

There was a vine on Karolin that would sometimes take a tree in its embrace just as ivy does, grow up it and round it and cling without doing the tree any injury; but if the vine were cut away from the tree, the tree would die.

It seemed to Le Moan that Taori was like the tree and Katafa the vine.

She was right.

Seldom enough, yet every now and then you find in this wilderness of a world, amidst the thorns of hate and the poison berries of passion and the dung of beasts and the toadstools of conjugal love, a passion pure and unselfish like the love of Katafa and Taori. Who moreover, above most other mortals, stood apart in a world there was no room for little things—where the sky was their roof and the ocean their floor and storm and war and cataclysm, halcyon weather, and the blaze of a tropic sun their environment, where the love that bound them together had, woven into it—after the fashion of the rope of Rantan—their past.

The thousand little and great and beautiful and terrific things that made up their past, all these were woven into the passion that bound them together.

To cut this bond, to separate them forcibly one from the other, was death.

In hot climates, in the tropics where the convolvulus grows so rapidly that the eye can all but see it grow, people can die quickly of love. Death grows when released with the fountain speed of the rocketing datura and the disruptive fury of corruption.

Dick cut away from Katafa was going to die. It was not only the cutting away, but the manner of it, that made his case hopeless.

Not only was he cut away from Katafa, but he was also divorced from his environment. His universe had consisted of Palm Tree and Karolin, the sea that held them, the sky above them: Katafa—nothing more.

Then Palm Tree had vanished and Karolin had been taken from him and nothing was left but the great vacant world of the sea, that and the grief for the loss of Katafa.

He was going to die. He was dying. His very strength was killing him.

You sometimes find that—find that the power of a powerful man can be turned in against itself by grief or by disaster or disease.

He was going to die, as Aioma said, and Le Moan knew it.

He was dying because Katafa had been cut away from him.

The sound of the bow-wash and the sound of the sea as it washed past the counter, and the creak of rope and spar, kept saying all this.

"Taori is dying because Katafa is no more with him—no more with him. . ."

Meanwhile the island grew.

And now Aioma, cheered by the sight of this bit of land, began talking to Poni in a high-pitched voice. But Le Moan did not hear or heed what he said.

So, Taori was going to die. And it was for this that she had taken him away from Katafa. She had taken him away to have him to herself and he was turning into a dead man. To save him from death she had given herself up to Peterson, to save him from death she had killed Carlin and risked being killed by Rantan, and yet he was going to die.

She could hear now the faint and far-away breathing of the surf on the reef ahead mixed with the words of Aioma to Poni; and now harsh and complaining and sudden and near came the call of a gull; a land gull, flying as if racing them.

"Taori is dying because of Katafa—Katafa—Katafa," cried the gull, and Le Moan following the bird with her eyes let her gaze sweep back to the deck where Taori was lying, half leaning, the sun upon his bare back where the vertabræ showed and the ribs.

And louder now came the breathing of the surf on the reef, heavy like the breathing of a weary man.

"All life is weary and full of labour," sighed the surf, "and there is no more joy in the sun—and Taori is going to die because of Katafa."

"Katafa," creaked the cordage to the foam that went sighing aft.

The wind freshened and the main sheet tautened and the great sail bellied hard against the blue, the schooner lifting to the swell crushed into it with great sighs and long shudders like the sighing and shuddering of a dying man, and the atoll leaped larger to view, the palm trees standing clear of the water above the coral and the visible foam.

"The palm grows, the coral waxes, but man departs," whispered the wind, repeating the old rede of the islands; and now the lagoon showed through the break and Le Moan, watching and knowing that there, should they enter that lagoon, Taori would find his last home beneath the palm trees, scarcely knew of the terrible battle raging in the darkness of her mind—knew only that she was all astray, helpless, useless, pulled this way and that between two opposing forces great as the powers of life and death; whilst louder now came the sound of the surf, louder and deeper and more solemn, till once again she was on the beach of Karolin, the stars were shining, the little conch shells whispering and chirruping to keep the evil spirits away, for Uta Matu the king was dying and his breathing came from the house like that.

Then, suddenly, with the cry of a dreamer awakened from some terrible dream, flinging out her arms to thrust away the dark spirit that had all but seized her soul and the body of Taori, Le Moan flung Poni from the wheel, seized the spokes and the schooner, checking, turned, her canvas thrashing and clawing at the wind.

Turned—the island wheeling to the port quarter and the main boom flogging out with Aioma and Poni hauling at the sheet; turned and held, close hauled and steering for the west of north.

"Karolin," cried Le Moan, "Aioma, the sight has come to me—the path is plain."

"Karolin!" cried Aioma. "Taori, the spell is broken, we are free and the net of Le Juan torn asunder and the spears of Uta blunted."

HENRY DE VERE STACPOOLE

VIII

What Happened to Rantan (conclusion)

S afe hidden amongst the bushes he listened. It would take a full hour yet before the schooner could make the break, yet he listened as he lay, his rope beside him, his mind active as a squirrel in its cage.

They would search the atoll, they would hunt amongst the bushes—yet they might miss him.

Should they find him! His dark mind took fire at the thought, wild ideas came to him of escaping into the lagoon, boarding the schooner, seizing a rifle and turning the situation. He was a white man, a match for a hundred kanakas if only he could get a foothold above them, a rifle in his hands. In this he was right, as he had slain the women who had him safely bound, so had he the possibility in him to meet this last attack of fate, free himself, and dominating and destroying, make good at last.

Time passed, the reef spoke and the wind in the trees, but from the outer sea came nothing. He peeped through the bushes, getting a view of the reef line to northward. By now surely the topmasts of the schooner ought to show close in as she must be, yet there was nothing.

He came out of the bushes like a lizard, stood erect and then came cautiously towards the higher coral where his outlook post was; literally on hands and feet he crawled, inch by inch, till the sea came in view and then he crawled no longer. He stood erect.

Far off on the breezed-up sea the schooner close-hauled was standing away from the island.

Rantan could scarcely grasp the fact before his eyes. She had been making for him and now she was standing away.

She had not been searching for him, then. Was she after all the *Kermadec* or had he been mistaken?

Her shape, her personality, that patch on the sail—well what of that? Other ships had patched canvas besides his schooner. He had surely been mistaken.

As she dwindled dissolving in the wind, his hungry eyes followed her.

How fast she was going, faster than the *Kermadec* could sail close-hauled.

He watched her till she was hull down, till her canvas showed like a midge dancing in the sea dazzle, till it vanished taken by the round world into the viewless.

Then he came back to the trees.

Just as the ship had gone from the sea, so had his dream ship gone from his mind, taking hope with her, leaving him to his utter nakedness. He went to the old canoe that he had abused and vilified in his hour of triumph; the sun had enlarged the crack, the forward outrigger pole had worked loose with the tossing in the swell, there was no paddle.

Yet she could talk to him, telling him of Nanu and Ona and their dead children, and of Carlin and Peterson, and beyond that of Soma and Chile and many a traverse to the beginning of that great traverse of his life.

He wished to be done with it all.

With the going of hope, the fact of his nakedness had seized him again.

It had never quite left him; the feeling of being without clothes had tinged even his dreams, he had fought against it and put it by, but it always returned, and now that hope had departed it was back and in a worse form. For now if he did not fight it hard, it was taking the form, not of discomfort and a sense of want, but of uneasiness, the terrible excitable uneasiness that the stomach can produce when disarranged—stomach fear.

He fought it down, returned to the trees and found that his worry about the ship and his own position had quite gone; he was worrying about nothing, for he was at grips with something new, something born of his naked skin and his stomach that had been feeding on uncooked food for so long, something that had been making for him for weeks, something that threatened to rise to a crisis and make him run—run—run.

Dropping to sleep that night he was brought awake by something that hit him a blow on the soles of his feet; twice this happened and when he slept he was hunting for his clothes, and when he awoke it was to face another blue day, a day lovely but implacable as a sworn tormentor.

He walked the beach in his nakedness.

The gulls had begun to jeer at him now. Up to this they had left him severely alone, treating him with absolute indifference, but they had found him out at last; they were laughing at him all along the reef, talking about him and every now and then rising above the trees to look at him.

HENRY DE VERE STACPOOLE

This idea held for a little and then passed, and he knew that he had been the victim of a delusion.

The gulls were quite indifferent to his presence.

Now amongst the trees and close to the waterside stood a gigantic soa with rail-like branches projecting like limbs across the sand and one big branch standing at right angles from the trunk some fifteen feet up.

Lying now amongst the tree shadows, and listening to the gulls' voices that had become normal, and the long roll of the unending breakers and the whispering movements of the robber crabs, Rantan fixed his eyes on this branch and saw himself in fancy swinging from it at the end of a rope, free of all his trouble, naked no longer. The rope he had woven and which was lying amongst the bushes had tied itself to the branch in his imagination.

He saw himself rising, hunting amidst the bushes and coming out of them with the rope in his hand; climbing the tree, fixing the rope to the limb, making the noose in the free end, placing the noose round his neck, dropping—kicking the air—dangling.

At noon a great gull sweeping across the lagoon from the leeward to the windward beach, seeing the dangling figure, altered its line of flight as if deflected by a blow, and a high-going burgomaster, seeing the deflected flight of his brother in hunger, circled and dropped like a stone to where Rantan was dangling and dancing on the wind. A naked figure yet capable, had the schooner put in, of boarding it by night, seizing command by treachery, sailing north and sweeping Karolin, for such is the power of the White Man. But Rantan was dead, slain by the action of Le Moan in putting the schooner about. This was the third time she had sacrificed herself for the sake of Taori, the third time that she had countered danger and death with love.

IX

The Green Ship

L e Moan steered. Tireless and heedless of time as when she had brought the schooner first to Karolin, she kept the wheel all that day and through the night, giving it over to Poni for short intervals, whilst Dick slept.

She had given life back to him and it was almost as though she had given him her own life, for the world around her had become as the world wherein ghosts move; disembodied spirits, not dead but no longer connected with earth.

Before setting eyes on Taori, she had lived on the southern beach of Karolin, lonely, cut off with Aioma and the others who had no interests beyond the interests of the moment; as she lived so might she have died neither happy nor unhappy, without pity and without love or care for the morrow or thought of the past.

Then Taori had come, not as a man but as a light greater than the sun, a light that struck through the darkness of her being, bringing to birth a new self that was his—that was he.

She had braved death and the unknown—everything—only to find herself at the end face to face with death, and death saying to her "He is mine—or Katafa's."

Like the woman who stood before Solomon, she had to choose between the destruction of the thing she loved and the handing of it to a rival to be lost to her forever, to see its arms clinging to another, and its love given to another, and its life becoming part of the life of another; and she chose the greater sacrifice, not because she was Le Moan, a creature extraordinary or supernormal, but just because at heart she was a woman.

A woman, acting, when brought to the great test, less as an individual than as a part of the spirit of womanhood. The spirit changeless through the ages and unalterable. The spirit so often hidden by the littleness of the flesh, so seldom put to the heroic test, so absolutely certain in its answer to it. For when a woman really loves she becomes a mother even though she never may conceive or produce a child.

Aioma, who had slept through the night on his belly on the deck, spread like a starfish, awoke as the sun was rising.

Poni was at the wheel—Le Moan had gone below. The cabin had no fears for her now, and she had said to Poni, just as the sun was rising and pointing into the west of north, "You will see the lagoon light there."

Dick, by the galley, was still sleeping, Tahuku and Tirai were the watch.

The beauty of that sunrise on that blue and lonely sea, beyond word or brush, was unseen by Aioma.

"It will be over there," said Poni, pointing ahead. "It does not show yet." Aioma went forward and stood looking into the northwest. No, it did not show yet nor would it show till the sun was twice its diameter above the horizon. Aioma, listening to the slash of the bow breaking the water and fanned by the draught from the head sails, having swept the sky found his eye caught by something far across the sea and right in their course. It looked at first glance like a rock but at once his bird-like eyes resolved it into what it was—a ship, an *ayat*, but with no sail set.

The canoe-builder glanced back along the deck past the sleeping figure of Dick to the figure of Poni at the wheel, then he turned his eyes again upon the far-off ship, and now in the sky to the north above and beyond the ship lay something for which he had been on the lookout— the lagoon light of Karolin, almost imperceptible, but there just in the position where Le Moan had said it would be.

The something he had waited and longed for, but spoiled, almost threatened, by this apparition of a ship.

Aioma wanted to have nothing more to do with ships; this traverse in the schooner had turned him clean back towards canoes; for days past, though he had said no word on the matter, all his ancestors had been hammering at the door of his mind shouting, "Aioma, you are a fool, you have forsaken the canoes of your forefathers for this *ayat*, and see how it has betrayed you, and why? Because it is the invention of the white men, the cursed *papalagi* who have always brought trouble to Karolin. If we could get at you, Aioma, we would stake you out on the reef for the sharks to eat. You deserve it."

He had said nothing of this because Aioma never confessed to a fault.

Well there was another *ayat*, blocking the way to Karolin and sure to bring trouble.

Civilization and trouble had come to be convertible ideas in the mind of this old gentleman who although he did not know the English word that represents greed, brutality, disease, drink, and robbery dressed in self-righteousness, had sensed the fact that the white man always brought trouble.

Well, there it was straight before him heading her off from Karolin. What should he do? Turn and run away from it? Oh, no. Aioma, who had fought the big rays and who was never happier than when at grips with a conger, was not the person to turn his back on danger or threat, especially now with Karolin in view.

This thing lay straight in his path, as if daring him, and he accepted the challenge; they had the speak sticks, there were eight of them not including Le Moan and if it came to a fight—well, he was ready.

Without rousing Dick, he called the fellows up from below, pointed out the ship and then stood watching as she grew.

Now she stood on the water plainly to be seen, a brig with canvas stowed as if in preparation for a blow. If any canvas had been set it must have been blown away by the wind, for she showed nothing but her sticks as she lay rolling gently to the swell.

Tahuku, who had the instinct of a predatory gull coupled with the eye of a hawk, suddenly laughed:

"She is empty," said Tahuku, "she has no men on her. It is a dead turtle, Aioma you have called on us to spear."

Aioma hit by the same truth ran and roused Dick, who on waking sprang to his feet. He was renewed by sleep and hope, a creature reborn and as he stood with the others he scarcely noticed the ship, his eyes fixed on the light of Karolin.

Poni at the wheel called Le Moan and she came up from below and stood watching whilst the brig, now close to them, showed her nakedness and desolation beneath the burning light of morning.

Old-fashioned, even for these days, high-pooped, heavily sparred and with an up-jutting bowsprit, her hull of a ghastly faded green rolled with a weary movement to the undulations of the swell, revealing now the weed-grown copper of her sheathing, now a glimpse of the deserted deck. There were no boats at the davits and as the current altered her position, giving her a gentle pitch, came a sound faint against the wind, the clapping of her deck-house door.

Aioma turning, ran aft and stood beside Poni at the wheel giving him directions. The canoe-builder, urged by his ancestors and his hatred of the *papalagi*, had evolved an idea from his active brain and Dick, who had let his eyes wander from the brig to the far-off light of Karolin, heard suddenly the thrashing of canvas as the steersman brought the schooner up into the wind.

Aioma was going to board the *ayat*. He was shouting directions to Tahuku and the others—they ran to the falls, the boat was lowered, and in a moment he was away, shouting like a boy; scrambling like a monkey when they hitched on to the broad channel plates he gained the deck and stood looking round him.

Aye, that was a place! Bones of dead men picked clean by the birds lay here and there, and a skull polished like a marble rolled and moved and rotated on the planking to the pitch of the hull, the clicking of the lax rudder chain, and the clapping of the deckhouse door.

He had brought his fire-stick with him and its little bow, from the deck of the schooner. They watched him as he stood looking about him. Then turning, he darted into the deck-house.

He was there a long time, perhaps ten minutes, and when he came out a puff of smoke came after him. Holding the door open, he looked in till another puff of smoke garnished with sparks, hit him in the face, then having done a little dance on the deck and kicked the skull into the starboard scupper, he dropped into the boat and came back to the schooner, singing.

The boat was hoisted in, the schonner put on her course and the smoking brig dropped far astern, but Aioma, still flushed with his work and victory, heeded nothing.

He sat on the coaming of the saloon skylight singing.

He sang of the bones of the dead men and the skull he had kicked and the *ayat* he had fired and the cursed *papalagi* whose work he had destroyed; then, with a great whoop he curled up and went asleep, undreaming that the *papalagi* might yet have their revenge, and Dick, to whom Aioma and the ship astern flaring horribly in the sunlight were as nothing, watched from the bow the steady growing beacon of Karolin in the sky.

There was Katafa.

His soul flew ahead of the schooner like a bird, flew back and flew forward again calling on the wind, and the wind, nearing, strengthened, so that a little after midday the far treetops of the southern beach came to view and now, faint and far away, the song of the great atoll.

Birds flew to meet them and birds passed them flying towards the land and as the sun began its downward climb to the water, the break began to show away on the port bow and Le Moan, pushing Tahuku, who was at the wheel, aside, prepared to take them in.

For only Le Moan knew the danger of the break when the tide was ebbing as now.

The waters were against them. It seemed the last feeble effort of fate to separate Dick from the being he loved.

The vast lagoon was pouring out like a river, it was past full spate, but the swirl was enough, if the helmsman failed to drive them on the coral.

Now they were in the grip of it, the schooner bucking like a restive horse, now steady, now making frantic efforts to turn and dash out to sea again—Aioma in the bow crying directions, Le Moan heeding him as little as she heeded the crying of the gulls.

Now they had stolen between the piers. The break on either side of them seemed immensely broad and the grand sweep of the outgoing water lit by the westering sun showed with scarcely a ripple to where it boiled against the piers: gulls in flight above it showed as in a mirror, yet it was flowing at a six-knot clip.

The schooner with every sail drawing seemed not to move, yet she moved, turning the mirror to a feather of foam at her cut water and a river of beaten gold in her wake. The piers dropped astern, the current slackened, the lagoon was conquered and lay before them a blaze of light from the beach sands to its northern viewless barrier.

Katafa was sleeping. She who slept scarcely at all by night and whose eyes by day were always fixed towards the sea, was sleeping when the voice of Kanoa roused her:

"They come, Katafa, they come!"

Raising herself on one hand, she saw the sunset light through the trees and the form of Kanoa making off again to the beach his voice drifting back to her as he ran:

"They come, Katafa, they come!"

Then where the whole village was waiting, she found herself on the sands, the lagoon before her and on the lagoon the schooner bravely sailing in the sunset blaze, the sails full and now shivering as, curving to her anchorage, the wind left them and the rumble of the anchor chain running out came across the water, rousing her to the fact that what she saw could not be, that what she saw was a ship, but not the ship that had taken Taori away, the ship she had watched and waited for till hope was all but dead and life all but darkness. It could not be. It could not be that she should return like this, so sure, so quietly, so real, the dream ship that held her heart and soul, her love, her very life.

The boat putting off now was a phantom, surely, and Taori as he sprang on the sands and seized her in his embrace was unreal as the world fading around her, till his lips seized her up from twilight to the heaven of assurance.

"Taori has come back," cried the women, forgetting him as they turned to the men who were standing by the boat—unheeding Le Moan who stood, her work done, a being uncaring, seeing nothing, not even Kanoa, crouched on the sands half dead with the beatitude of the vision before him.

X

Aripa! Aripa!

L isten!" said the wind.

From her place amidst the trees where Le Moan had settled herself like a hare in its forme she heard the silky whisper of the sands and the voice of the beach and the wind in the leaves above bidding her to listen.

Far-away voices came from the mammee apple where the men of the schooner and their wives were making merry, and now and then, the faintest thing in the world of sound, a click and creak from Nan on his post above the house where Taori lay in the arms of Katafa.

To Le Moan all that was nothing. She had banded death in exchange for Taori, all her interest in life, all her desires. She had not even the desire to destroy herself. The fire that had been her life burned low and smouldered; it would never blaze again.

"Listen!" said the wind.

Something moved amidst the trees—it was Kanoa: Kanoa, his heart beating against his ribs, his hands outstretched touching the tree boles.

She saw him now as he came towards her like a phantom from the star-showered night, and she knew why he came, nor did she move as he dropped on his knees beside her—all that was nothing now to Le Moan.

Since the night when he had saved her from Rantan, he had been closer to her than the other men of the schooner, but still only a figure, almost an abstraction.

Tonight, now, he was a little more than that, as a dog might be to a lonely person, and as he poured out his heart in whispers she listened without replying, let him put his arm around her and take her lips; all that was nothing now to her whose heart would never quicken again.

The wind died, day broke, and the wind of morning blew.

Joy and the sun leapt on Karolin. Joy for Katafa who came from the house to look at a world renewed, for the women whose husbands had returned, for the men, for the children. Joy for Kanoa, his soul shouting in him, "She is mine, she is mine," and for Aioma, the lust of revenge and destruction alive and dancing in his heart.

He had killed the green ship; this morning he would kill the schooner; the cursed *ayat,* that he had yet loved so dearly only a week ago, was doomed to die.

He hated it now with an entirely new and delicious brand of hatred and if he could have staked it out on the reef for the sharks to devour, so would he have done.

It had given him the scare of his life, it had all but snapped him away from Karolin, it had caused ancestral voices to rise cursing him for his folly and treachery towards his race; it had brought up visions of the Spanish ship, the brutal whale men, Carlin, Rantan, and the whole tribe of the *papalagi,* it was theirs and it had got to die.

Besides, it was going to give him the chance to set fire to things. He was still licking his chops over the firing of the green ship and the joy of incendiarism was about to be recaptured.

It was the last blaze up of youth in him. He called the village together and explained matters.

The *ayat* was accursed. His father, Amatu, had explained it all in a dream, commanding him, Aioma, to attend to this matter. The thing had to burn; if it did not burn worse would befall Karolin.

"Burn, burn, aripa, aripa!" cried the boys.

"Aripa!" shrieked the women, the men took tongue and the cry went up like the crackle of flame.

Katafa listened, loathing the schooner. The cry went up from her heart.

Dick stood dumb. Dumb as a man hesitating before cutting away the very last strand connecting him with his past. Dumb as a man about to renounce his race, though of his race and of the civilized world from whence he had sprung he knew nothing—nothing save the fact of the cannon-shot of the *Portsey* long years ago the white-led Melanesians of Palm Tree, the ruffianism of Carlin and Rantan and the rage in his own breast for adventure that had nearly separated him forever from Katafa.

Then, suddenly, he joined in the shout.

"Aripa! aripa! aripa!"

Forgetting his chieftanship he raced with the others to help to push off the boat bearing Aioma to his work.

Then he stood with Katafa watching. Near them and beside Kanoa stood Le Moan.

They watched the canoe-builder clamber on board like a monkey, they saw him dancing on the deck like a maniac insulting the ropes and spars, then they heard the ship's bell go clang-clang, as he made her talk for the last time.

He vanished down the foc'sle and came out escorted by a cloud of smoke, down the hatch of the saloon from whose skylight presently a blue-grey wreath uprose and circled on the faint breeze.

Then he was on deck again and away in the boat, and the schooner was burning fore and aft.

Wreathing herself in mist that cleared now to show two tall columns of smoke rising and spreading and forming spirals on the wind, red flames like the tongues of hounds licking out of the portholes, flames that ran spirit-like about the old tinder-dry deck. The main boom was burning now, the topping lofts were snapped, flames curling round the masts like climbing snakes, and now, like the rumble of a boiler, came the rumble of the fire as it spread in her, breaking through bulkheads, seizing the cargo and splitting the decks.

The sandalwood was burning and the incense of it spread across the lagoon to the white-robed congregation of the gulls wheeling and giving tongue above the reef; burning and blazing till the decks gave utterly and the crashing masts full sheeted in flame like tall men tumbling to their ruin amidst the roar of a burning city.

The flames devoured the smoke and the sun devoured the flames, forty-foot jets that leaped tongue-like sunwards, fell and leapt again. The great conflagration gave no light; it roared, and the consuming wood, pine and deal, teak and sandal filled the air with the sound of bursting shells and the rattle of musketry, but the sun of that blazing day ate the light of the flames so that they showed stripped of effulgence, stark naked; ghosts, cairngorm coloured, wine coloured, spark spangled, illuminating nothing.

And now the port bulwarks, breaking in one piece from the stern to amidships, fell in a blaze and the anchor chain, running out, broke from its attachments and she was adrift miraculously on the flood, now low to the break, now broadside, as the current took her—blazing as she drifted, pieces of her ever going, dipping now by the bow, slipping from sight in a veil of steam as the water rushing in fought the fire and the fire fought the water and was killed. And now there was nothing but driftwood so far out as scarcely to be seen, and a tiny cloud that vanished and a perfume of sandalwood that lingered in the air, ghost-like. . . gone.

XI

The Green Sickness

All that remained of her was the boat, the lesser of the two boats which Aioma had saved for the moment.

The island was without a single canoe, and he intended to build one as swiftly as might be for the fishing; that being done he would destroy the boat and so obliterate the last trace of the cursed *papalagi*.

So he set to work and the work progressed, Le Moan helping with the others. She worked at the making of the sail, Kanoa helping her, happy, ignorant of her utter deadness to all things, yet sometimes wondering.

Sometimes this woman he had taken to his heart seemed indeed a spirit or a lost soul as she had seemed to him that time before the killing of Carlin; always she was remote from him in mind, untouchable as the gulls he had chased as a child on Soma. Yet she was his and she let him love her,—and "Time," said the heart of Kanoa, "will bring her arms around me."

Her strangeness and indifference increased his passion. A child and yet a man, he moved now in a wonder world, he was always singing when alone and there was something in his voice that made it different from the voices of the others, so that when the women heard him singing in the groves they said "That is Kanoa."

And despite his happiness in her and his love for her and his embraces, despite the joy of new life that filled Karolin and the beauty of the nights in which Taori and Katafa walked together on the reef, never once did the desire come to Le Moan to destroy herself—all that was nothing to her now.

She had torn out her heart and nothing else mattered, even life.

"And tomorrow or next day," one morning said Aioma, "the canoe will be ready and we will burn the lesser *ayat* as we burned the greater. Ah hai, what is this, the reef is lifting before my eyes—Look you, Tahuku!"

But Tahuku saw nothing. The reef was solid as of old and the sun was shining on it and he said so.

The canoe-builder shut his eyes and when he opened them again the reef had ceased to lift, but he was weary. Bells rang in his ears and his hands were hot and dry and now after a while and towards midday one of the *papalagi*—so it seemed to him—had seized him from behind and tied a band round his head, screwing it so tight that he would have screamed had he been an ordinary man.

He lay on the ground, and as he lay a woman, one of the wives of Poni, came running, panting as she ran.

"I burn, I burn!" cried the woman. "Aioma, my sight is going from me; I burn, I burn!" She fell on the ground and Katafa running to her raised her head.

Aioma turning on his side tried to rise but could not, then he laughed.

Then he began to sing. He was fighting the *papalagi* and killing them, the Spaniards of long ago and the whale men and Carlin and Rantan; his song was a song of victory, yet he was defeated. The white men had got him with the white man's disease. Measles stood on the beach of Karolin, for the green ship with its cargo of labour had fallen to measles and Aioma in boarding it had sealed his doom.

It was Poni who guessed the truth. He had seen measles before—and now, remembering the ship, he cried out that they were undone, that the devils from the green ship had seized them and that they must die.

He had no need to say that.

Aioma lasted only a day, and the lagoon took him; by then the whole population was down, all but Taori, Katafa, Le Moan and Kanoa.

Kanoa had taken the disease at Vana Vana many years ago and was immune; the others, saved, perhaps, by the European blood in their veins, still resisted the disease.

The people died on the coral or cast themselves burning into the lagoon and were seized by the sharks, who knew.

And to Le Moan as she watched them, it was not the green sickness that did the work, but she herself.

She had brought this curse on Karolin. She had brought the schooner and the white men, she had taken the schooner to meet the green ship; it was the mother of her mother, Le Juan, who was reaching through her to slay and slay. Aioma in a lucid interval before he died had seized her by the hands and told her this, but she had no need of the telling of Aioma. She knew. And she watched, helpless and uncaring. She could do nothing, and the people passed, vanished like ghosts, died like flies, whilst the wind blew gently and the sun shone and the gulls fished and dawn came ever beautiful as of old through the Gates of Morning.

XII

The Release of Le Moan

One night, when the disease seemed past and only ten people were left of all those who had watched the burning of the schooner, Le Moan, sleeping by Kanoa, was awakened by Katafa.

Katafa was weeping.

She seized Le Moan by the hands and raising her without waking Kanoa, led her to the house above which Nan still stood frizzy-headed in the moonlight.

In the house on a mat Dick was lying tossing his head from side to side and talking in a strange tongue.

Talking the language of his early childhood, calling out to Kearney whom he had long forgotten, but whom he remembered now.

The green sickness had seized Dick—resisted for days and days it had him at last.

Le Moan stood in the doorway and the moon looking over her shoulder lit the form on the mat, the reef spoke and the wind in the trees, but she heard nothing, saw nothing and for a moment felt nothing.

Taori was lying on the mat talking in a strange tongue, turning his head from side to side.

Then, as a person all but drowned, all but dead, comes slowly back to life and comes in agony, Le Moan began to feel the world come round her once more, the world she had known before she tore her heart out.

Taori was going to die. And the heart she had torn out was back again and the love that had filled it.

Taori was going to die—to die as the others had died and as surely, and as certainly through her who had brought this curse on Karolin and through whom the hand of Le Juan was still striking.

So great was the power of this thought that it fought with and overcame the passionate desire to fling herself on her knees beside him and take him in her arms; so great was its power that it almost drove the thought of him away before the crowding recollections it brought up of her own disastrous history in which she had brought evil to everyone. To Peterson, to Rantan, to Carlin, to Poni, to Tahuku—Tirai, all whom she had touched or come in contact with. To Aioma—and lastly to Taori.

Taori is going to die—*Ai amasu Taori*—the wind sighed it above him, it came mixed with the sobbing of Katafa and the voice of the beach with the rumbling voice of Taori himself, talking, talking, talking, as he wandered on the reef of memory with Kearney in a land that knew not Katafa.

Ai amasu Taori—and she dared not bid him goodbye; to save him she must go, leave him untouched, for the net of Le Juan was not yet torn, nor the spears of Uta blunted.

Even to look at him was fatal, yet she could not tear her eyes away.

Ai amusu Taori—a great breaker on the coral cried it to the night and broke the spell and turned her towards the weeping Katafa.

"Oh, Katafa," said Le Moan, speaking in a voice clear but scarcely above a whisper, "Taori will not die—I go to save him; the nets are spread for him but I will break them, I the daughter of Le Jennibon, the daughter of Le Juan."

Even as she spoke the voice from the house quieted.

"I who have brought this evil." Katafa heard her voice, not knowing what she said, for the change in the voice of the sick man was speaking to her.

Gliding into the house she lay down beside him, her cool hand upon his brow.

Le Moan turned to the beach through the trees. Night rested on Karolin and the moon showed the sands far stretching and filled with the silky whisper of the wind.

Far to the right lay the canoe all but completed, to the left the boat of the schooner. Le Moan came to the boat.

The tide was full, almost touching the keel, it was a light boat, the sands were firm, and evil though it was, it could not resist her. Afloat, with an oar, she drove it out, and raising the sail shipping the rudder, gave the sail to the wind.

The wind was favourable for the break, the ebb was beginning to run, all things were helping her now because she had conquered. Death could do no more against her for she was his.

To the right lay the moonlit sands of the southern beach from which she had sailed that morning with Peterson and with a dread in her heart that she did not feel now; before her lay the widening break with the first ebb racing through it to the sea, a night-flying gull cried above her as the breakers loudened on the outer beach and fell behind her as the wind and tide swept her out to the sea.

Far out, beyond return by drift or chance, she brailed the little sail, unstepped the mast and cast mast and sail to the water, cast the oars to the water, and lying down gave her soul into the hands of that Power through which her mother's people had gained release when, weary of the world, they chose to turn their faces from the sun.

Northwest of the Paumotas men talk of a vast atoll island half fabulous, half believed in. Ship masters have sighted a palm line by day reefless because, steer as they will, some sort of current has never allowed them to raise the reef and by night the pearling schooners have heard the breathing of a beach uncharted, and always on the sound a wind has followed blowing them away from the mysterious land.

Karolin—who knows?—the island of dreams, sealed by the soul of Le Moan to the civilization that the children of Lestrange and their child escaped from; a beach that the pleasant sunshine alone lights for me; where Aioma shapes his logs and where I watch, undisturbed by the noise of cities, the freshness we have lost and the light that comes alone through the Gates of Morning.

The End

A Note About the Author

Henry De Vere Stacpoole (1863–1951) was an Irish novelist. Born in Kingstown, Ireland—now Dún Laoghaire—Stacpoole served as a ship's doctor in the South Pacific Ocean as a young man. His experiences on the other side of the world would inspire much of his literary work, including his revered romance novel *The Blue Lagoon* (1908). Stacpoole wrote dozens of novels throughout his career, many of which have served as source material for feature length films. He lived in rural Essex before settling on the Isle of Wight in the 1920s, where he spent the remainder of his life.

A Note from the Publisher

Spanning many genres, from non-fiction essays to literature classics to children's books and lyric poetry, Mint Edition books showcase the master works of our time in a modern new package. The text is freshly typeset, is clean and easy to read, and features a new note about the author in each volume. Many books also include exclusive new introductory material. Every book boasts a striking new cover, which makes it as appropriate for collecting as it is for gift giving. Mint Edition books are only printed when a reader orders them, so natural resources are not wasted. We're proud that our books are never manufactured in excess and exist only in the exact quantity they need to be read and enjoyed.

Discover more of your favorite classics with Bookfinity™.

- Track your reading with custom book lists.
- Get great book recommendations for your personalized Reader Type.
- Add reviews for your favorite books.
- AND MUCH MORE!

Visit **bookfinity.com** and take the fun Reader Type quiz to get started.

Enjoy our classic and modern companion pairings!